AIR HOSTESS
DIARIES

Cyrus M Gonda | Smrity B.

AIR HOSTESS DIARIES

Cyrus M Gonda | Smrity B.

EMBASSY BOOKS

www.embassybooks.in

Air Hostess Diaries

Published in India by :
EMBASSY BOOK DISTRIBUTORS
120, Great Western Building,
Maharashtra Chamber of Commerce Lane,
Fort, Mumbai - 400 023.
Tel : (+91-22) 22819546 / 32967415
Email : info@embassybooks.in
Website: www.embassybooks.in

ISBN 13: 978-93-80227-70-2

Acknowledgements

A big thank you to Prof. Mohammed Osaid Koti for overseeing the entire production values of this book.

Our sincere thanks to Sonia Panjwani and Ritesh Koli of Vcreate Design Agency, who have designed the cover and also provided the sketches and diagrams which appear throughout the book.

Thanks also due to Sohin Lakhani and Varsha Shah of Embassy Publishers for having placed their faith in this project.

And of course, thank you to the courteous and brave personnel of the cabin-crew profession, to whom this book is dedicated.

Happy Reading and Happy Flying.

Air Hostess Diaries

Preface

This diary, while being a work of fiction, reflects the trials and tribulations of the courageous and glamorous women and men engaged in the business of caring after passengers as they fly across the world from one destination to another. The world of the air-hostess is a unique world; no other career can compare with it.

This diary traces the story of one such fictional air-hostess, right from the time she completes her aviation course, secures a flying job, finds a paying-guest accommodation, attends her first airline party, helps out her colleagues who fall prey to male attention, and matures into becoming a confident woman of the world.

This diary will make you laugh, it will make you cry, it will make you realise that there is a world beyond the world in which you are living.

Scores of friends and acquaintances have added to our existing knowledge base of the inner functioning of the aviation industry and have helped us derive a realistic understanding of the life of an air-hostess. The incidents and insights they have shared, coupled with the personal experiences of the co-author Smrity, (herself a senior air-hostess with a leading International Airline), have been distilled into this entertaining and educating portrayal.

The first in a series of books to soon follow, this diary provides a kaleidoscopic view into the wonderful world of commercial aviation through the eyes of our heroine, Preity Singh.

Air Hostess Diaries

Date : 25th May

Life in the Big City

My Dear Diary
How've you been? It's been a year since I last opened your pages. I'm reeeeally sorry for not speaking to you for so long. But there's a good reason for it. I wanted to test myself and see if I could survive without YOU, my best friend, in this big city of Mumbai. Sort of like a challenge to see how tough I could be. To see if I could stand without support. And I managed it. Now, Dear Diary, let me tell you what I've been doing in this past one year.

As you know, I've been here in Mumbai since the last one year doing my air-hostess course. Good news for you. I've just completed it. AND, I've got a job.

Dear Diary, I'm now no longer just plain Preity Singh.

I'm now Preity Singh – AIR HOSTESS.
So much has happened in this one hectic year, Dear

Diary, and I'm simply dyyyying to share it all with you.

You've been my good friend over the years. In some ways, you've been my very bestest friend. In the sense that I've shared everything with you, things that I haven't ever shared with anyone else.

Sometimes I wonder why I feel you've been my best friend for such a long time. I guess it's because you've never ever let me down.

You never laugh at me.

You never misunderstand me.

You quietly listen to all that I have to say and accept me just as I am – A normal young girl, with the normal mix of overconfidence and self-doubts. A girl who feels up in the skies one day and a little down on the next.

You've shared my sorrows, my joys, my most private thoughts, my innermost feelings.

You've been and become a part of me. You and me are now **in-sep-ar-able.**

You're the very first person I told my feelings about Manoj to. Me and him were in school together. And then we both went to junior college together. You remember Manoj, right? Back home in Dehradun?

But back in school, me and him were just ------ well, friends. And then, when both of us went to junior college ----- that's when we started spending more time together. That's when we discovered that we had a lot in common.

And, Dear Diary, do you remember when I came to you and shared with you that ---- first ---- kiss? Ahhhhhhh. What a day that was. Manoj had taken me to see a movie back in Doon after our eleventh standard exams. He held my hand throughout the movie. It was such a romantic experience for a young teenager like me.

There were stars on the screen but I had stars in my eyes.

I came out of the theatre in a daze.

After the movie, we walked home through the Doon bazaar. That's the first time any boy ever held my hand in public. I felt so very grown up. So mature.

And just before we reached my cottage, in that quiet lane with leafy trees shading the evening sun, he held me close, brushed his lips over mine, and then, as if embarrassed by his own boldness, wished me a hurried 'bye' and walked off.

But I had so wanted him to stay. With that kiss, he had awoken something in my heart that I never knew existed. I knew that I'd crossed a certain line. In some way, I didn't know exactly how, but that faint brushing of lips signified a turning point in my life.

Sighing gently, I watched him fade away into the distance, and then I went home, walking on cloud nine. Mom asked me how the movie was.

Movie? What movie? I hardly remembered any of it. But I hurriedly gave mom a vague answer, and then rushed to my room, Dear Diary, to meet **YOU**. To imprint the memory of that beautiful day and that first kiss on your pages for eternity.

Maybe some day, my kids will read of my feelings after that first kiss, and laugh.

Maybe they won't laugh, but they'll understand.

Maybe, they'll never read about it.
Maybe ---- maybe ---- I may never **HAVE** any kids.
I'm so ----- confused.

The memory of that warm feeling and that cold December day in Dehradun confuses and excites me even now.

So, I'm going to do what I always do when I'm confused and excited. I'm going to confide in you. I don't know exactly why, but confiding in you always gives me peace of mind.

And helps me to clarify my thoughts.

Well, Dear Diary, as you know, after me and Manoj finished our twelfth standard exams, we took different routes on the path of life. He went off to Delhi to pursue his engineering, which had always been his dream. I was so proud when he secured admission into a good engineering institute in Delhi. Imagine – having an engineer for a husband.

And I pursued **MY** passion of coming to Mumbai to do a one year, full time in-flight cabin-crew course and hopefully get a job as an air-hostess after that.
But before we both left Doon for our chosen destinations, we promised each other that no matter what the physical distance between us, our minds and hearts would always remain one. And soon, once we'd finished our education, we would return to Doon, our lovely hometown, get good jobs in Doon or some-place nearby, and spend a blissfully happy life together with our kids. We sealed our promise to each other with a deeeeeeep kiss.

How honest we were when we made these promises to each other.

But how naïve we were too.

Today I've learnt that life doesn't always work out the way we plan it. In fact, most times it doesn't.

Distractions cannot always be overcome.

Distances cannot always be ignored.

But **BECAUSE** most times we **DON'T** always get what we

planned for, that's why the few times we **DO** get to fulfill our dreams, the results seem even sweeter.

Well, I came to Mumbai from Doon with only **one** friend, Dear Diary, and that is you.

Of course, I soon made many new friends at my cabin-crew institute. We were a batch of thirty bright, cheerful, enthusiastic kids, and since it was a full-time course, we spent a lot of time together. It was a close knit batch, but even within that batch, I made five special friends.

There were six of us who were almost always together. Ajay, Aneesh, Ashfaque, Sunaina, Kaveri and me. We never planned to form the group with this mathematics of three plus three in mind. It just sort of worked out that way.

All of them were pleasant individuals, and I gelled well with each of them. I'll describe a few of them to you as we go along.

You know **me** well, Dear Diary, so I hardly need to describe **myself** to you.

The mirror tells me that I'm slim with an athletic build, quite tall, fair, have thick black hair which I wear fairly short, have an attractive face with s-l-i-g-h-t-l-y Chinky features, a straight nose, large bright brown eyes, and high cheekbones. Sounds like quite a good package, doesn't it?

What the mirror **DOESN'T** tell about me is that I'm basically honest, (sometimes to the extent of being downright blunt), hard working, outgoing, loyal, stubborn (at times), love enjoying myself but at the same time I know my responsibilities. I looooove my family. I'm tough, yet sensitive, and I looove animals, which is why I'm a vegetarian by choice, though I eat eggs. (I loooove cakes and cheese omelets, so I haven't been able to give up eating eggs as yet, but one day I will.)

Coming back – I faithfully kept in touch with Manoj in Delhi, speaking to him at least once a day. Sometimes he used to call up, and sometimes it was I.

We never kept count who called more often and whose turn it was to call next.

I've seen that petty issues like these lead to ego hassles and end up destroying even the best of relationships, and I was determined not to let our relationship go down the drain for such petty reasons. We couldn't speak for long very often, as both of us were busy with our studies and our new friends, but at least we kept in touch regularly, and that kept the fire within us glowing.

Now let me tell you where I've been putting up since this last one year in Mumbai. This city is **soooo** different from our lovely hill station. I don't know **why** people bother to stay in such large cities, so far away from nature and good clean air.

But I guess it is jobs and careers which lure and force people to settle down in large groups. And once these groups reach a certain largeness, they just keep growing larger and larger. That's the best way to describe a giant city, I think.

Accommodation is a big hassle in Mumbai, Dear Diary, and I was fortunate to be staying with my aunt's family, who are settled here. (My aunt is my mom's younger sister – my *maasi*.)

She's a housewife, and her husband is a senior executive with an export firm. They have a son who's working abroad and a daughter who is a few years younger to me, studying in the ninth standard. They have a three bedroom apartment in the suburb of Andheri, which was convenient for me, as my aviation institute was located nearby.

Fortunately I was given a bedroom to myself. As their son was overseas, I stayed in his vacant room. Aunt and uncle shared another, and my little cousin Nisha had the third bedroom.

Although they gave me a roof over my head, I could sense that somehow my aunt and uncle were not too happy about me staying with them. Mainly because they wanted their daughter, (my cousin Nisha), who was a brainy and beautiful young girl, to grow up and become a doctor or a chartered accountant or something equally brilliant.

Nisha had always been a very studious girl, but ever since I'd come to stay with them, she'd started dreaming about becoming an air-hostess herself. Every evening when all four of us sat down together for dinner around ten o'clock, Nisha eagerly enquired from me how my day had gone, and what new stuff I'd learnt at the air-hostess training institute that day.

She liked to put on my training uniform jacket and move around the house, which really irritated her mom. She started dropping hints to her parents that she would be very happy if she could fly off to different places and see the world. This didn't please my aunt and uncle at all, and I could plainly see that.

I tried giving Nisha hints that since she was so brilliant and good at her studies, (unlike me who was an average student), she should make good use of her brains and study as much as she could.

But she'd already got the sky in her eyes.

It would be quite difficult to get the idea of becoming an air-hostess out of her fertile young mind.

Not that I felt that she shouldn't become one.

It's a great career. A **super** career. And I'm all for it. But different strokes for different folks. One size does **not** fit all.

To avoid the glares of my aunt and my uncle, and to avoid being around too much so as not to influence Nisha, I started spending less time at home with them and more time with my group of five friends. Since none of the five were from Mumbai city, and apart from me, none of the other five were staying with relatives but were putting up in different student hostels near the institute, none of us needed to be at home before nine in the evening, which is the time the girl's hostels wanted them back.

So although our institute timings were from 9 to 4, Monday to Friday, I used to end up telling my aunt that we had extra lectures till eight in the evening almost daily, and that extra lectures were being held the whole of Saturday as well.

I didn't **like** doing this, Dear Diary, because as you know me well, I don't like lying.

But I didn't consider what I was doing as lying. What I told my aunt wasn't hurting anyone.

I considered it as buying peace.

I guess my aunt knew that I wasn't speaking the truth about the extra lectures, but since she was happy that I spent as little time at home as possible, she didn't question me too much. She just taunted me once in a while when I was extra late in coming home, which according to her would be anything after nine thirty in the evening. "I just hope that all this extra studying you're doing is going to get you a job as soon as you finish the course. Your folks spent a lot of money in sending you here for your studies", was her constant refrain, which I ignored.

With this arrangement, everyone was happy, Dear Diary, apart from poor Nisha, my little cousin, who got to spend less and less time with me. She hardly got any chance to query me about what new stuff I'd learnt each day about being an air-hostess.

I felt guilty about not spending time with her, and was extra nice to her on Sundays when I spent the day at home, just to make up for being away from her throughout the week. I felt really sorry for the poor kid. She was a nice, sweet girl and I felt that her parents ought to let her follow her own heart, not make her follow their heads. But that's something that wasn't in my hands to decide.

So all in all, I wasn't too popular in that household, though I never let my mom know it. It would just have upset her.
The end result of all this was that I became closer and closer with my special group of friends from the airline institute. And as I'd mentioned, since in our group we had three good looking, attractive girls, and three smart, charming guys, you can well guess what happened.

I didn't **MEAN** for it to happen, Dear Diary.

Over a period of time, we all just sort of paired up.

It just ------sort of --------happened.

I was still loyal to Manoj and spoke to him regularly in Delhi. But my conversations with him were gradually becoming more and more mechanical.

Now let me tell you about Ajay, Dear Diary. Ajay, the guy from our group of six, who'd become **MY** special friend, was from Vizag. Ours was a typical *aloo-paratha* meets *idli-sambhar* story.

Ajay was a charmer. The epitome of tall, dark, handsome and athletic.

If I was the North pole, he was the South. He had perfect white teeth and there was a lovely dimple on his chin which appeared each time he smiled, (which was very often.) A twinkle in his deep, dark eyes completed the gorgeous package.

He stayed at a boy's hostel very near our institute. He was great fun to be with, and the other girls in our batch were envious of me as I ended up spending so much time with him.

I couldn't help it if Ajay was equally attracted to me as I was to him.

Me and Ajay sat next to each other in class and even did our homework assignments together while sitting in a coffee shop till late most evenings.

That's where we started spending more time looking into each other eyes more often than we were looking into our study notes.

In the beginning, the other two couples which had formed our special group of six regularly joined us, but increasingly me and Ajay found some excuse or the other to be alone somewhere by ourselves.

We were already ten months into the course, and had just another two months to go before completion.

By now, my conversations with Manoj in Delhi were getting less frequent. We hardly spoke to each other even twice a week, and spoke for barely a few minutes each time we connected. Our conversations were becoming more and more forced, difficult and mechanical.

Soon, our conversations barely went beyond –

"So what you been up to?"

"Nothing much. What **YOU** been upto?"

"Oh, just busy. How's your engineering going?"

"Not too bad. Have some projects coming up for submission. How's **YOUR** cabin-crew course going?"

"Oh, good but hectic. So what'd you have for lunch today?"

"Was busy, so just grabbed a sandwich. What did **YOU** have for lunch today?"

That was getting to be the general trend of our conversations, Dear Diary, and after an embarrassing pause in the conversation when both of us were stuck for something to say, one of us would mercifully put an end to the misery by saying – "Well, gotta be going. Speak to you soon."

"Bye."

I didn't fail to notice, Dear Diary, that since the past few weeks, our conversations had been ending with a vanilla flavoured – **"Speak to you soon"**, rather than the initial – **"I love you a lot"**, which had later downgraded to – **"I love you"**, which then degenerated to – **"Miss you"**, and now it was just plain – **"Speak to you soon"**.

To tell the truth, I had got a little too absorbed in the atmosphere of the city.

Mumbai, to me, was now reality.

Delhi, where Manoj was studying, was almost a universe away for me. And I guess I was a galaxy away for him by now.

Not that I wanted to be disloyal to Manoj, Dear Diary. I tried my best to keep our relationship going. I reeeeally did. But it takes two to make a relationship work, and Manoj could equally share the responsibility for it fizzling out.

So my evenings towards the end of the course were spent mostly in the many coffee shops that dot the landscape of the city of Mumbai. When not chilling in a coffee shop, we were shopping at Linking Road or sometimes at Fashion Street, or we would be seen soaking in an evening show at a multiplex. Although I had constantly heard so much about the famed pubs and night life of Mumbai, I hadn't yet visited a single pub or spent a night out. For one thing, I could never be home later than ten, because that's the time I had to join my aunt, uncle and Nisha for dinner once uncle came home from work around nine thirty. (Working life in Mumbai's tough on timings.)

And secondly, I'd promised myself not to visit a pub even in the afternoon until I got myself a job. I make these promises to myself and stick by them so I find it easier to reach my goals by having a little treat waiting for me when I achieve them.

It's my method of self-motivation and it works wonders for me. It also helps in building my will-power, something which every girl should be developing, along with going to the gym to develop her figure.

Well, by now we were nearing the end of our year long course, and each one of us was gearing up for our job interviews. This was what we'd all been waiting all year for. The most coveted jobs of course, were the flying jobs, which were everyone's dream. But our institute had instructed those of us who didn't get a flying job to take up a ground job with an airline, and at least get a foothold into the aviation industry.

I was as nervous as all my other batch-mates when I went for my first interview with Princess Airways. Maybe my nervousness showed in the interview. Or maybe they felt I just wasn't good enough to fly for them. Although I felt my interview had gone reasonably well, I wasn't selected.

Ajay, on the other hand, was picked up immediately by the same airline. But then, Ajay is a combination of a terrific personality, charm and super-confidence, all rolled into one. A Super-duper Man.

I was very proud of him for getting the job, but I felt sad that we wouldn't be working alongside each other in the same airline. It would have been **so** much fun, undergoing our airline training together, and then being on the same flights once in a while. This now meant that I'd be seeing less of him, although hopefully we'd still both be based in Mumbai. That is of course, provided I got a job here.

I went for my second interview with another airline. I didn't clear that either.

But I did some self-introspection and identified where I was lacking from my two failed interview experiences, gathered confidence, and I cleared my third interview a week later with Lion Air.

I WAS NOW OFFICIALLY AN AIR-HOSTESS.

Of course, my six week training with the airline and my probation period were still to follow, but **I had got a flying job.** That was the main thing.

I won't bore you with details of my interview, Dear Diary, but I can tell you that I was confident, answered all the questions well, and the interview got over some time before lunch.

The first thing I did on leaving the interview room after I'd been told I had been selected was to call mom. She was **DE- -LIGHT--ED.**

I could visualise her joy as she shared my happiness. Not that my becoming an air-hostess was her ultimate dream for me, but whatever I'd wanted to achieve in life, she's always been so supportive.

Dad was at work, and she promised to tell him the good news as soon as she could. Then she put *Dadi* on the line. *Dadi* can't hear very well, so I had to yell out the news. But hey, that wasn't a problem as I felt like yelling out the good news to the whole world.

So I shouted at top volume – "***Dadi*, mujhe air-hostess ki naukri mil gayee**."

After yelling this out, I stared around hesitantly as I realised that I was on the footpath just outside the airline office where I'd given my successful interview, and people nearby were staring at me. I smiled at them self-consciously, and they smiled back, understanding how excited this young girl must be feeling, at the news she'd just yelled out to her *Dadi.*

A stranger passing by even came up and congratulated and wished me – "All the best." I thanked him gratefully. Who says Mumbai is not a friendly city?

The next call I put through had to be to Ajay.

I confess I didn't even **think** of informing Manoj back in Delhi the good news.

I called Ajay thrice and he kept cutting me off.

I called a fourth time, and he picked up. Before I could say a word, Ajay hissed from the other end – "Idiot, if I'm cutting your call, can't you understand I'm busy?" and then he cut off.

He said this in a low tone, but so viciously, that I immediately burst into tears.

My joy turned sour.

He'd never, ever, used that tone of voice with me before.

Maybe I'd been thoughtless in not realising he'd been busy with his airline training, but he could at least have told me that he was busy in a pleasant tone.

My face crumpled up. I cried softly, although I try never to cry in public.

I know it wasn't such a big deal that I had to cry over it, but his tone pierced my happy heart and punctured it when I was least expecting to be hurt.

I just couldn't help it. Ajay had sounded so horrid. Almost as if he hated me.

Then a thought struck me.

After Ajay had been selected for his airline job around ten days ago, he hadn't been so keen to call me up and tell me he'd been selected as I had been to call him. In fact, although his interview was to have got over by eleven in the morning, I'd eagerly waited till around six in the evening for his call telling me how his interview had gone. I waited and waited, thinking that maybe his interview had been delayed, after which I just couldn't wait any longer and I'd called him. His phone had been engaged. I called again after ten minutes and it had still been engaged. Fifteen minutes later he'd called up and casually told me he'd got the job. I asked him what time his interview had got over, and he'd vaguely replied that it got over some time after lunch.

At that time, I hadn't given it much thought. I was just too happy for him that he'd been selected.

But now this.

I started to think.

And I didn't like what I was thinking, Dear Diary.

Was he tired of me?

Was there someone else?

There was definitely no shortage of girls who'd have liked to latch on to Ajay, but he'd never shown any signs of being interested in anyone other than me. But then, I realised I'd just been close to him since the past six months. That's really not enough time to know a person inside-out.

That's one mistake our generation makes, Dear Diary. We get attracted to people TOO quickly. On surface appearances.

We don't take the time to peer below the skin in depth. To understand the entire personality of the other person. Their values, their priorities, their sense of right and wrong.

Then another thought struck me. In the last couple of weeks, ever since the course got over and we'd all started going for interviews, (he'd got his job within a few days of the course getting over), me and Ajay been meeting up less and less.

Oh, he always gave me a convincing reason for not meeting up. Like – "Hey Preity, I've got to prepare seriously for my interview. And you know that when I'm around you, all I can do is think of you. Even when you're not around, I have a tough time keeping my mind off you. So we better stop seeing each other so much for a couple of weeks till we've got our jobs, okay?"

At that time I was flattered that he thought about me so much. Which girl wouldn't be thrilled to hear a handsome guy say that all he could do was think of her? After all, I'm only human, Dear Diary.

And, it also told me that Ajay was really serious about his career. That's another thing that any girl admires in a guy.

Especially in **HER** guy.

By now, I was possessively thinking of Ajay as **MY** guy, although we hadn't really committed anything to each other. But from the amount of time we'd been spending alone with each other during the last few months, the implied message had been clear, at least to me.

But now that I started to put together these small negative signals I'd been receiving since the last two weeks, doubts started to emerge in my mind.

Thinking these thoughts, I walked into a nearby coffee shop and sat down at a table. The waiter smilingly asked me which coffee I'd like.

"Just get me any cold coffee on the menu and don't bother me with any more questions", I snapped, immediately regretting my rudeness.

"I'm really sorry", I told the waiter. "I didn't mean it. I was just upset over something."

"That's all right, Ma'am", he said cheerfully. "I'll get you a nice, cold coffee with ice cream. It's perfect for this hot weather. You'll enjoy it."

"Thanks", I smiled, "and I'm sorry."

Was this the sort of rude outburst that I'd have to be facing myself from upset passengers when I asked them if they'd like coffee, I wondered to myself. I just wished I'd be able to handle such outbursts of temper from irritable passengers half as well as this waiter had handled mine.

While I waited for my coffee to arrive, I deliberately let my mind go blank. The coffee appeared on the table. Mechanically, I ate the ice cream on top before starting to sip the chilled coffee through the straw.

It tasted good, but I wished I'd asked for something hot to drink. It would have put some warmth into my chilled bones. Although the temperature in Mumbai city at that moment was over thirty-five degrees centigrade and sizzling, the moment Ajay had snapped at me so viciously, I'd felt myself go cold from the inside.

I finished my coffee, paid the waiter, left him a large tip to make up for the shameful way I'd snapped at him, and walked out aimlessly on to the hot street. Since I just had on a white shirt tucked into a navy blue knee length skirt which I'd worn for the interview, I was glad of the warmth the sun gave me.

I didn't know what to do now that I'd finished my coffee.

I didn't feel like going home to face aunt.

I didn't feel like meeting any of my other friends nor asking them how their job hunt was going. Ajay had been one of the first in the batch to get placed. Most of us were still on the lookout for jobs and going for interviews whenever we got an opportunity.

I looked at my watch. It showed just twelve-thirty in the afternoon. I had a whole day to kill by myself. As I mentioned, most of my other batch-mates were appearing for some interview or the other themselves and were occupied.

I decided to take a train to Churchgate, the heart of Mumbai, stroll around the shopping area in Colaba near Churchgate, and spend the day by myself, maybe doing some shopping for costume jewelry, which I love.

First, I had a bite to eat at a small restaurant in Colaba.

Then I bought a pair of flat sandals from a roadside stall and decided to immediately put them on. I removed the heeled shoes which I'd been wearing for the interview and put them in my handbag. Now at least I could walk in comfort, and I planned to do a lot of walking that day, till I tired myself out.

I also purchased a pair of cute earrings from a street stall. I didn't even bargain, but just paid the guy what he asked. That should tell you the state of my mind better than anything, Dear Diary.

Imagine. Me – Preity Singh – passing up an opportunity to bargain.

Unthinkable under normal circumstances. I recall how the shop-keepers back home in the Dehradun bazaar used to shudder when they saw Preity Singh approaching.

I had no idea how the time passed. No idea how the afternoon flew by, till at six, dad called up from home to congratulate me. He'd just returned from work and mom had given him the news. He was delighted and blessed me with all success. I was overwhelmed at hearing a friendly voice over the phone. I tried to speak cheerfully to him so he couldn't feel the catch in my voice, as I struggled to keep it normal. Fortunately, he felt that the crack in my voice was due to the joy I must be feeling at having got the job of my dreams. I promised dad I'd visit them for a short trip back to Doon as soon as possible. Mom came on the line and spoke a few words as well, and then hung up.

Preity Singh was alone once again in this big city.

I continued moving around aimlessly in the back-lanes and by-lanes of Colaba.

I didn't even realise that it was now past seven and the sun had set. My mind and my innermost thoughts had anyway been pretty dark throughout this supposedly happy day. So whether it was sunny or dark outside, I hardly noticed.

I came back to my senses with a jolt, when in a quiet and secluded back-lane where I was aimlessly strolling, not looking left or right, a man came out suddenly from the shadows and propositioned me. I felt as though a bucket of cold water had been poured over me. I shook myself out of my lethargic state, and hastened my steps, not daring even to turn back to see the guy's face. Almost at a run, I reached the safety of the main road; the crowded Colaba causeway.

I took a firm grip on myself and sternly told myself that I couldn't keep walking the streets aimlessly now that it was dark. Guys were starting to think I was a hooker. How humiliating. And scary.

I took a deep breath, decided once again to call Ajay, and try and speak to him.

I prayed, and called.

Joy, oh joy, Dear Diary.

This time he picked up and started off with – "I am **SOOOO** sorry Preity. I was juuuuust about to call you. I was in a training session and we'd been strictly told to keep our phones off. My phone was on when you called because I was expecting an important call from papa, and I was

24

afraid the instructor would get upset. But I shouldn't have spoken to you the way I did. Where are you now? Would you like to meet up for dinner? We haven't seen each other since I started my training a week ago."

Did I want to meet up?

I suuuuure did.

I'd like nothing better.

But why did I get that tiny feeling that he wasn't quite speaking the truth? Anyway, I was so happy at hearing that we could have dinner together, that my mood-meter neatly swung from a low of zero to a high of hundred.

I was aware that his training was being conducted at Andheri. That's where my aunt's house was, anyway. I was currently at Colaba, which is about forty-five minutes journey away from Andheri by train, which is the fastest mode of transport in Mumbai.

I told Ajay I could meet him someplace in Andheri in about an hour, and that I'd loooove to have dinner with him. I hope I didn't sound too eager, Dear Diary. I didn't want to appear to be a pushover for anyone, even Ajay.

We fixed up a place to meet, and I reached there in just over an hour. Although the train was jam-packed as it was peak-time for the office travelers returning home, I was too happy in my thoughts to be really disturbed by the uncomfortable journey.

I was on top of the world.

I had a job as an air-hostess.

I was going to have dinner with the bestest, handsomest guy in the whole world.

What more could a girl ask for?

Ajay was waiting outside the restaurant where we'd fixed up to meet. He'd already reserved a cozy corner table for two.

I first hugged him, overjoyed at seeing him after ages. (It **seemed** ages to me Dear Diary. In love, even a minute apart is an eternity.)

We both congratulated each other on our new jobs. Then we had a leisurely dinner, just chatting comfortably, catching up on events in our lives in the last two weeks. It was such a pleasant atmosphere, that time simply flew.

We finished the meal, he paid the bill, and we walked out.

Once on the street, we walked close to each other, holding hands.

Suddenly, the topic of how I felt he'd been avoiding me came up.

Or rather, I **brought** it up.

I made my feelings felt. I just couldn't help it.

You know how it is, Dear Diary. When two people are still getting to know each other, they are on their best behavior.

They're testing the waters.

They're politeness personified.

Even if they feel hurt, they don't show it, but laugh it off and keep their emotions hidden.

But the moment a certain barrier is crossed, and a sort of intimacy is established, a comfort factor comes in, which makes the people feel they can now take off their masks.

It's like wearing a new pair of shoes, Dear Diary. We're very conscious and careful of these new shoes for the first few days. We avoid stepping with them in a puddle of water. We brush off the slightest stain or mark and try our best to keep them spotlessly clean.

But after that initial honeymoon period is over and done, the special treatment is over too.

I always feel human behavior is very strange in that way.

I feel that relationships should **improve** with time.

The concern we show for each other's feelings and the basic politeness and courtesy we show each other when we're relative strangers should actually **magnify and enhance** once the relationship grows, and not be reduced and forgotten.

It is unfortunate that because of such initial false politeness, in most cases, people fall in love with a mask, not the real thing.

You can't keep a mask on all the time; all your life. You wouldn't be able to breathe. You'd suffocate. So once the honeymoon is over, the masks come off, and the true colours show. And sometimes, the true colours aren't very pretty to see.

I really feel it's better to just be yourself in every way right from the beginning with every person you meet. Then if the other person **does** fall for you, **he falls for the real you**, and he knows what he's getting.

But society has its own weird and peculiar rules, and these are the rules of relationships.

Guess somebody needs to change the rules; then perhaps the game of love would make more sense.

Anyway, coming back to me and Ajay. In the infant stages of our relationship, I'd never have **dared** to raise my voice against Ajay and blatantly tell him that I felt he'd been ignoring me.

But that's just what I did after dinner while we were having our romantic walk.

It's very much like a mom whose kid has run away. The mom is frantic with worry, and the moment she finds the kid, she may give it a tight slap before kissing it. That's just the way my emotions worked. I was so upset with Ajay for having caused me this heartache, that I bluntly questioned him why he had seemed so cold and distant ever since before his job interview two weeks ago.

He hesitated a bit.

Then he started to explain.

His explanation stunned me
.
By the manner and tone in which I had questioned him, he may have thought I had a hint what was going on, and that's why he stumbled out with the truth. My casual

questioning brought out a hornet's nest of revelations which I'd never even dreamed off and which I wish I'd left alone.

He was silent for some time as if thinking of how to put it. Then he began by bluntly saying that he had a confession to make.

I listened, not knowing what was coming.

He said it was good I'd brought up the issue, as he didn't want to keep anything from me.

He continued by saying that it had always been his dream to get a job with the airline he was now working for.

I nodded. I knew that.

He went on that although he knew he had a good chance of getting the job, the airline he'd applied for only had a few vacancies. And although he knew he was good, the competition for those few vacancies was pretty stiff.

Also, there were fewer vacancies for guys than there were for girls anyway, and he was desperate enough to do anything to secure a job there. That's where the problem began.

That's where problems always **do** begin, don't they, Dear Diary? With that word called **desperation.**

Anyway, as soon as Ajay had heard about the vacancy, he'd begun his networking activity, and through a friend, he got the information that a senior lady in that airline had a huge say in the selection process.

This friend of Ajay's knew this lady, having been selected by her for a cabin-crew job the previous year, and he agreed to put Ajay on to her. His friend told him that there was only one hitch – if it could be called a hitch.

The lady was in her late thirties, and quite good looking, though slightly overweight. She was a divorcee. She came from a very wealthy, aristocratic family. She owned a posh apartment in a premium locality where she stayed all by herself.

She had an affinity for sophisticated, good looking young guys, and enjoyed their company. This sort of thing happens in the corporate world like it does in other walks of life. People in positions of power do sometimes take advantage, is what his friend told Ajay.

The long and short of it was, his friend saw Ajay as exactly the type of guy this lady preferred, and offered to introduce him to her before the selection process commenced. Ajay is not stupid, and he knew what that offer meant. He was okay with it, as the world today follows the policy of – 'You scratch my back, I scratch yours'.

So his friend arranged for Ajay to meet this lady that very evening in a five-star hotel coffee shop.

They met, and she obviously liked what she saw. Ajay was honest with me, and he admitted to me that he liked what he saw as well.

She ordered coffee for both of them and they started chatting. She put her cards on the table and asked Ajay if he would be willing to spend some time over the next month with her – giving her company.

She openly told him that if he agreed, the job he wanted would be his. He didn't need to worry about that once she'd given her word. But her conditions were crystal clear.

Ajay's friend had told him that a month was all that he'd have to spend with her, as she soon tired of the same guy, and there was no shortage of young, willing guys looking out for a job in an airline, at the same time getting to live in five-star comfort for a few days with a good looking lady.

Ajay told me that to be honest, until that point of time he really had not made up his mind whether to agree to these terms. He told me that each time he thought of agreeing to the arrangement, my face came before his eyes and held him back. He said that as if he meant it, not just to please me. I believed him.

But he said that when the lady herself put forth the proposal and assured and guaranteed him his dream job, he succumbed and agreed on the spot.

She was pleased, and said that although she wasn't on the interview panel, she would put in a strong word to the people who would be on the panel, and they owed her a few favours. The job would be done.

"Let's celebrate the beginning of your career in aviation" – she told Ajay. She took him to her apartment and he left the next morning, fascinated at the lifestyle of the rich and the powerful.

He had felt too guilty to call me up, and had given me the excuse that he was busy with interviews. Actually his interview was scheduled a couple of days down the line, and the lady had already taken care of it. So the next two days he had spent just lazing around, and stayed the nights at her apartment.

His interview rounds were a cakewalk, and he was in. She'd kept her word.

Once he got the job, he was told that his training would be starting off in another four days. But he'd lied to me that his training would be starting off immediately, as he still didn't have the heart to face me. In the meanwhile, he spent another couple of nights at her place, before his training commenced.

Now, his training had been on for eight days, and she'd already tired of him, much earlier than his friend had predicted. Some new guy was servicing her and Ajay was free to move on. She hadn't told him this, obviously, but he guessed that a replacement had been found for him, the way she'd suddenly stopped asking him to come over since the last three nights.

In his heart of hearts, Ajay was relieved, as what he'd been doing had made him feel cheap and used. He had always dreamed of being a purser, never a gigolo. Now at last he could get back to meeting me with a clear conscience.

That's why he'd wanted to catch up with me over dinner, and being basically an honest person, he'd wanted to share all these happenings with me.

The problem he had faced was how to tell me all this without hurting me terribly. That had been his dilemma.

I'd listened to all this in complete silence, Dear Diary.

Complete, stone-cold, icy silence.

We were still walking along the road. The only difference between us since he had started on his tale and now that he'd ended it, was that somehow in the middle of it all, I had sub-consciously left off holding his hand.

I was hurt, yes. But not broken.

If this had happened to me a year ago, I would have been shattered. But in this one year that I'd spent on my own in the city – Preity Singh had changed. I knew better now how most men's minds worked.

Being honest to myself, I felt I couldn't even really blame Ajay. After all it's not that the two of us were officially a couple.

He had every right to take decisions which would help him further his career.

What he had said had definitely hurt me, but his being so honest about it was like balm to my soul.

I took his hand in mine again and told him it was all right. I could understand how bad he was feeling about the whole thing.

I knew that he hadn't been lying when he said he was glad he was rid of her. His obvious relief at being out of her clutches was too genuine to be an act.

That's one thing I know about Ajay – he can't lie with a straight face. He may be charming, but he's pretty honest as a person.

We walked on silently for some time, alternating the pressure on each other's hands.

I told him it was all right. I forgave him.

Then I asked him a question which no girl could resist asking under such circumstances.

I hesitantly asked him if he missed her.

He laughed.

He asked me if he wanted an honest answer.

When he said that, my heart grew cold; but I said of course I did.

He told me that if that was the case, he'd be honest.

He said there was no sense in honestly disclosing everything and then messing it up by lying about ten percent of the issue.

He said that if I meant whether he missed her physically, of course he did. "She was wild" – he said. Somehow, that hit me, hard. I didn't ask him to elaborate what he meant by that. It was too obvious. And painful

Sensing my hurt, he continued by saying that any guy would miss her physical presence. But when it came to feminity, womanliness and all the other qualities which keep a man attracted over a period of time, I was the only one for him. No one could top me for my good nature, my gentleness, my honesty and those things.

Although I knew that was an exaggeration, I was flattered.

Then he told me to forget about her, as he himself had forgotten about her.

He told me a story about an old monk and a young monk, who were travelling across the country. One of the rules of their sect forbade them from having contact with young women. The two monks came to a river, and a beautiful young lady was waiting there for someone to help her across. The elderly monk without hesitation carried the young lady across the river, left her on the other side, and then the old monk and the young monk went on their way.

An hour later, the young monk, whose mind had been disturbed by the entire episode, asked the elder monk how he could physically carry a beautiful lady when the tenets of their religion strictly forbade physical contact with the fairer sex.

The elder monk smiled and told the young monk – **"My son, I dropped her off long back. It is YOU who are still carrying her."**

This is how Ajay completed this wonderful fable.

"That's what I want you to understand, Preity", said Ajay, earnestly. "You've been really sweet and understanding about this whole thing. I doubt that I would have taken it so well had I been in your place. In fact I'm sure I wouldn't have been able to. **Now just forget about her and stop carrying her in your mind**. She means nothing to me. She used me and I used her. Now we're on our separate ways."

He paused.

"I want your way to be forever joined to my way, Preity", he said.

I felt a tingling in my heart that I'd never felt before, Dear Diary.

It was as though we were the first couple in love that the world had ever seen.

The moon shone down on us, bathing and blessing us in its glorious golden light.

I forgave him with all my heart.

I only hoped that I would never give him a similar reason in future to forgive me.

We walked and walked and walked. I felt I was walking on soft, puffy, clouds. My feet didn't seem to touch the ground.

Time stood still.

Or rather, it seemed to do so.

It never does, does it, Dear Diary?

As they say, time and tide wait for no man.

This was proved true, as in the middle of this blissful scene, my cell phone started to faintly play its tune through the confines of my purse. At first I couldn't understand what the sound was. I was so absorbed in my thoughts and the presence of Ajay, that the cell calling out from inside my purse seemed to be in another world.

It was Ajay who said, "Preity, your phone."

I hurriedly opened my purse, saw the number flashing, and groaned.

Who else?

It was my aunt.

God.

What was the time?

I was supposed to be home by ten at the latest.

We all had a family dinner at home together at ten as you know, Dear Diary.

I picked it up, prepared for a yelling, and was glad that Ajay was by my side.

The first harsh words that hit me were – "Where are you?"

I said I'd just finished dinner with a friend and was on the way home. As soon as I said that, I knew I'd blundered. I was supposed to be having dinner with them at home.

Then aunt started shrieking. She said they were waiting for me to reach home since ages, she had been calling me since the last half an hour and I hadn't the decency to pick up the phone (it must have been ringing since long in my purse and we hadn't heard it), and that they were all worried sick about me, and here I'd already finished my dinner and hadn't even bothered to inform them? Did I know what time it was?

I hurriedly glanced at my watch. It showed ten forty-five.

Oh God. Why had I been so careless? If I'd just called them up, then this wouldn't have happened, and I wouldn't have spoiled a brilliant evening for myself and for Ajay.

Ajay couldn't hear the actual words, but he guessed I was being given a blasting, and he held my hand tight in support.

The blasting continued. "I don't care in which part of the city you are, Preity Singh. I want you home within fifteen minutes or else - - - - - ."

That was it.

Ajay looked at me, concerned. "Trouble?" he asked.

I shook my head. "Nothing I can't handle", I said, making an attempt to smile. After all, why should Ajay's evening be spoiled because of my problems? I just requested him to drop me home as soon as he could. Fortunately, we'd been walking around the restaurant in circles and we were right near to where Ajay had parked his bike. We hopped on, and I reached home within twenty minutes of aunt having called up. That still made it a little past eleven o'clock.

The door opened before I could ring the bell. My aunt stood there, grim faced. My uncle was seated on the sofa, also wearing a solemn look. Nisha was nowhere to be seen.

"Sit down. We want to have a serious talk with you", said my aunt in a stern voice.

I sat.

"We've tolerated your nonsense long enough, only for one reason. And that's because your mother happens to be my elder sister."

"Who was that guy you were clinging to on the bike? The guy who dropped you and rushed off in such a hurry? Is this what your parents have sent you to this city for?" - was the first set of questions I was hammered with.

Evidently they'd been keeping a watch on the building entrance from the apartment balcony, which faced the road.

I **hadn't** been clinging to Ajay on the bike.

Not real clinging, anyway. Obviously I had to hold on to him so I wouldn't fall off, since I was wearing a skirt and seated with my legs at the side. But I saw no sense in arguing that point with my aunt.

The mind always sees what it wants to see, Dear Diary, and always believes what it wants to believe.

She had made up her mind to see the bad in everything I did, so the best thing I could do was to keep quiet and hear her out.

I just wanted to end this one-sided conversation, go to bed, and rush off to my dream world, flying high in the sky in my smart air-hostess uniform, serving coffee at thirty thousand feet to appreciative passengers.

But my aunt and uncle still had more to say. They'd waited a long time to say it, and they seemed determined to get their money's worth.

If not both of them, at least my aunt had a lot more to add. My uncle stood by her as though to give her moral support. Not that she needed it. She was going strong on her own steam.

"You listen to me Preity Singh", she continued. "And pay attention and look at me when I'm speaking to you. We have a daughter who we're doing our best to bring up in the right way in this difficult world. She's at a very impressionable age and I don't want her getting any weird ideas about how to proceed with her life. Before you came to stay with us, she was very focused on her studies. **We have great plans of making her something worthwhile in life, not just a waitress in the sky.**"

That hurt. That hurt me bad, and I couldn't help retaliating.

"Is that so?" I said. "Perhaps you haven't heard of something known as Dignity-of-Labour. You feel that only doctors and chartered accountants are worth knowing? **Well, let me tell you that without the tailors and the cooks and the waitresses you seem to look down upon, you'd be moving around nude and hungry.**"

I regretted the words even before they left my mouth.

I wished like anything that I could take them back.

But the damage was done.

I knew I'd get a tight slap for my outburst, and I knew I deserved it.

And that's exactly what I got.

A tight slap.

So the slap didn't surprise me.

It was the source of the slap that gave me a shock.

It didn't originate from my aunt, who stood as stunned as a statue at hearing these harsh home truths, and at having a mirror shown by me to reflect her proud and snooty attitude.

No. The slap came from my uncle, who till then hadn't said a word or participated in the entire scenario in any way.

"That does it," he said. "I've always been against the idea of you staying here with us, coming home at odd hours and being a source for the neighbours to gossip. They'll be talking the same language about our daughter soon, if you stay here any longer. At least until now, you've been coming home to sleep every night. Now that you've got a flying job, (mom must have called and told them about it), I suppose you'll get an excuse to be out at nights as well. You'll upset the orderly routine of this entire household, give everyone in the locality a juicy topic to gossip about, and be a lousy role-model for our Nisha."

He paused to take a breath and then went on. "You move out of our house as soon as possible. I'm giving you one week to find another place to stay, and in the meantime, you better learn to control your tongue when you speak to us. Ungrateful little wretch. I thought your airline training at least taught you to be polite with elders. **Is this how you're going to talk to your high flying passengers up in the sky?"**

Owww. That stung, Dear Diary.

Most of all because I knew he was right.

God. I try so hard. I really do. When will I learn to control my temper?

But right now, I didn't know whether to laugh or to cry.

Of course, the slap did hurt.

And finding a place to stay wasn't going to be that easy either. That worried me too.

But Oh, the joy of staying away from them. The joy of being by myself.

I just can't imagine that my aunt and my mom are sisters, Dear Diary. Oh, they do **look** alike, but that's where the resemblance ends. At the surface.

My mom is so sweet, genuine, helpful. And my aunt? Forget it. The less I say the better. I know I shouldn't be ungrateful, Dear Diary. She and my uncle have given me a roof over my head for a year.

But I guess it's time to move on now.

Anyway, coming back, Dear Diary.

The slap hurt, but I knew I'd asked for it. Even though I'd been provoked, I shouldn't have said what I said. She **is** an elder. And she is my mom's sister. One of my closest relatives in the world.

And if I can't keep my temper when an elder family member provokes me, what am I going to do at work, when passengers who are total strangers would possibly be provoking me each day?

I guess I still have a lot to learn.

Classrooms can't teach you everything.

Oh, they can give you the technical and theoretical inputs all right.

But when it comes to human skills, daily life is the best classroom.

But the lessons that daily life teaches you are worthwhile only if you learn from your mistakes and don't repeat them.

So I immediately apologised to my aunt and then to my uncle. I accepted that I shouldn't have been so late and should have kept them informed. I apologized for my rudeness.

I also thought over it for a moment and then told them I'd move out within a week if they could give me that time to find a new roof in this big city. I also thanked them for having taken care of me for a whole year.

"We'll talk about it tomorrow", said my aunt, recovering her power of speech which my earlier outburst had seemed to have taken away.

I joyously went to bed and had a sound sleep. The last thought before I dozed off was, that in ten day's time, I'd start my air-hostess training with an airline and also have a new room in a new home, all to myself.

With such happy thoughts, I dreamt happy dreams.

Date : 29th May

Well, Dear Diary,
There are many lessons I have learnt from my stay
in this city in the last one year, without having
mom and dad to look after me as they always have.

Life is different when you're on your own with no
mom and dad around. That's Lesson One. It's not
been all bad. I have learnt to be independent in
many ways.

Some people learn this early on in life by going to
boarding schools. Some like me learn it a little later.
But it's a lesson we all need to learn.

I've also learnt that you can be young only once.
Once responsibilities come onto your head, that's the
day you lose your youth. So my message is, enjoy
being young while you can. Don't misuse and
abuse your youth, but rather make the most of it.

Another thing I've experienced is that love doesn't
always last across distances, however hard you may
try to keep it alive.

I've also realised that you need to confide in your partner if you want your relationship to grow stronger. Good news can wait. Bad news can't.

I've learnt that while super-glue is excellent at putting most things together, it can't mend broken relationships.

I've also realised that the present and the future can keep you so occupied, that it's senseless to waste time thinking over the past.

Sorry, Dear Diary, got to go now. You have a great day and I'll see you soon with more inputs from the life of Preity Singh.

Date : 5th June

Pub Visit

Hello Dear Diary,
So sorry for being out of touch for a week. Hope you
haven't been too lonely without me around. I'm sure
you'll forgive me. I haven't forgotten you. It's just
that sooooo much has happened since we last met
and its kept me real busy, and now I'm simply
dying to tell you all about it.

I mentioned when we last met, Dear Diary, that
uncle and aunt gave me a deadline for moving out
of their house. They also made sure they told my
mom the reason for their decision immediately, so
they could get in their side of the story before I could
tell mine. About how my odd hours and wayward
behavior (according to them), was setting a bad
example for their daughter.

I really pitied their poor daughter. I really like that
kid. Too bad she's got such rigid parents.

Anyway, I spoke to mom and told her what had

actually happened. Of course, I realise I was partially to blame as well, and I didn't hide that from mom. I may be strong willed, Dear Diary, but I can accept my mistakes.

Mom knows me well and she knew I wouldn't do anything that would hurt or disappoint her or papa. I love them too much to do that. Mom also obviously knows her own sister well, and had realised that a clash between me and her sister was bound to happen sooner or later once we stayed under the same roof.

The advice mom gave me was sound as usual.

She reminded me to be grateful to aunty and uncle for all that they had done for me. She told me that my dad would have never sent me on my own to Mumbai as a student for a whole year if I hadn't been staying with trusted family members. So I owed my career as an air-hostess to my aunt and uncle. (I must confess I hadn't thought of it that way.) She requested me to apologise once more to them for my rude remarks.

I readily agreed, Dear Diary. It's no sin for a person to apologise even if both parties are at fault.

Mom told me to immediately start looking out for new accommodation and secure it as soon as possible. Although I still had a week to stay with my aunt and ten free days to go before I started with my airline training, mom reminded me that house hunting in Mumbai would be a killer task.

Mom also made me promise that I'd share my accommodation with other girls who were level headed and like-minded, and not heavily into the drug and party scene. Mom knew she could rely on me to stay in line and not cross extreme boundaries, but as a mother she still had a duty to caution me.

She told me she wouldn't be telling dad about these new accommodation hassles right now, as it would only make him hyper and dash down to Mumbai to help me in my house hunt. She had requested my aunt not to mention it to my dad either, till I'd secured a new accommodation for myself.

I now had seven days to finish this task.

I also told mom about me and Manoj drifting apart. She had known about me and him being close while back in Doon. I told her that we hadn't quarreled or anything like that. It was just that maybe we were not yet mature enough to keep a long distance relationship going.

I also told my mom about my losing my heart to Ajay. I tell my mom **e-v-e-r-y-t-h-i-n-g.** Along with you, Dear Diary, my mom is also my best friend.

I felt much better after I spoke to mom. Speaking to her always takes all the load off my mind. I hope it doesn't put all my load on to hers.

I now decided to take a couple of days break before I began house hunting, just chilling with Sheetal, Susan and Meena, three of my girlfriends from my batch, who'd also got jobs in different airlines and had a few days free as well before they started their training. Since they're all from Mumbai, they didn't have any housing hassles to worry about.

Ajay was busy throughout the day with his training, (which was now in full swing), else I'd have loved to spend the couple of days with him, just lazing around and exploring even more of this huge city.

But even without Ajay by my side, the two days that I spent with Sheetal, Susan and Meena were gorgeous.

We had real girlie type fun.

We saw two movies.

We gossiped.

We laughed over silly jokes.

We tried out different places to eat.

We shopped till our bags were full and our wallets were empty.

This time, I promised myself I'd keep an eye on my watch and be home by ten sharp in the evening. I didn't want mom to be disturbed with any more complaints about me, especially since these were the last few days I was spending with my aunt and uncle.

On the second day we girls spent together, (which was a Saturday), towards early evening, the girls suddenly decided to visit a pub.

This was the treat I'd promised myself once I got a job, (a pub visit), and I eagerly agreed to go along.

It was my first time ever in a pub, and though I wouldn't admit it to my friends, I was in awe of the atmosphere, the flashy outfits everyone had on, and the dense smoke that circulated all around.

The smoke had a sweet, peculiar smell, which Susan, a regular pub visitor, told me was the smell of *charas*, a common smell in most of the pubs in the city.

Once we were inside, I wished I'd put on something other than faded jeans and a long-sleeved tee-shirt, but then we hadn't known when we left home in the morning that we'd be visiting a trendy pub, where the young crowd came dressed in their best outfits.

When we went in, the place was already quite packed, (on Saturdays, the pubs in Mumbai get a crowd flowing in from afternoon onwards.) Music was blaring, and there was quite a crowd on the dance floor in the centre.

We located an unoccupied table and sat down. Susan ordered vodka for herself, the other two ordered gin. They asked me what I'd prefer to drink and I didn't know what to say.

I've never ever had alcohol in my life. Not that I'm a prude, but I just haven't tried it ever.

I decided to try it out.

After all, you can't enter a pub and not drink, can you, Dear Diary? I didn't want to look out of place. I left the choice of my drink to them. Susan ordered a gin and tonic for me. She said it was a beginner's drink. I couldn't wait to see how it would taste.

The drinks arrived on the table, along with a bowl of chips.

I hesitantly picked up my glass, sniffed it, and had a small sip.

Then I took a huge gulp.

I liked the taste and the pleasant feeling it gave me as it went down my thirsty throat. It burned slightly, but it was a pleasant burn.

"Hey, take it easy", said Sheetal. "Act sophisticated. You're supposed to make a drink last. It's not water, you know."

Embarrassed, I tried to act sophisticated. I had been sitting at the edge of my seat, absorbing the environment around me wide-eyed.

Now I reclined in my chair and attempted to look at home in the surroundings, as though I came here every day.

I casually stirred my gin and tonic with the stirrer and squeezed a little lime into it, emulating the other regulars around, who were totally at ease in these surroundings.

I loved the vibrant atmosphere and was closely watching the people moving on the dance floor. I wished Ajay was here with me. We could have had such a nice time, dancing the evening away.

While I was enviously gazing at the couples grooving to the music on the dance floor, a guy came up to our table and stretched out his hand towards mine. I instinctively got up and followed him on to the floor.

Well, Dear Diary, you know I've been to dances back home in Doon, but those dances had been organised by our school or college, with teachers all around supervising us youngsters. The presence of the teachers was enough to keep the dancing within certain limits.

But here there were no limits.
The dance floor was like an urban teenage jungle.

It was just like the scenes I'd seen on MTV.

The atmosphere was infectious and I was grooving on the floor with my partner. I didn't even know his name.

Just five minutes ago, he had been a total stranger to me. Come to think of it, he still was. But already I felt as if he and I were the only two human beings on earth.

I was nodding my head like a zombie to the beats of the trance music.

Already, my exertions were exhausting me. I gulped in breaths of *charas* filled smoke. My partner was executing some weird but skilful dance steps. He appeared to be totally oblivious to my presence. I was mesmerised, and just tried to keep up with his pace and rhythm.

Suddenly, he moved away, and another guy took his place.

This guy was keen on a more physical form of dance. He put one hand on my back, held my shoulder with the other, and rushed me into a weird mix of salsa, samba and God-knows-what-else, all rolled into one.

The floor was getting more packed now. The music changed, and the tempo became even faster.

Suddenly, I'd had enough.

My first drink, the electrifying atmosphere, the *charas* filled smoky air, the thumping music, and my strenuous gyrations on the floor with two different partners, all combined, made me feel close to fainting.

I released myself with some difficulty from my partner's grip, and bumping into a few other couples, stumbled to find my way back to our table.

Trying to locate the table in the near dark was like playing Blind-Man's Bluff. Feeling by instinct, rather than seeing, I reached our table at last. Only Meena was still seated there. Susan and Sheetal were by now on the floor, dancing up a storm.

Meena laughed at seeing my expression. "You're on your way to becoming a big city girl. Total **bindaaas**. Have another drink?"

I shook my head to indicate a 'No'.

I couldn't speak.

I was gasping for breath.

So this was what 'pubbing' was, I thought dizzily to myself.

I'd really enjoyed the dancing. The only regret I felt was that I wished it had been Ajay with whom I'd had my first dance in this city that I was planning on making my home.

I closed my eyes, absorbed the rhythm of the music in my skull, tapped my feet and nodded my head in time to the beats, and imagined I was with Ajay on the dance floor, his protective arms around me.

I wondered if I should call him and invite him over. It was only seven o'clock, and the evening was still young. I could comfortably be here for another two hours at least before leaving for home, and Ajay would have by now finished his training for the day.

I left the inner area of the pub, and walked out to the lobby, where I could at least make myself heard over the sound of the music if I made a phone call.

In the lobby, I observed the young crowd pouring into the pub, and noticed the fancy outfits the girls were wearing. I felt a bit out of place in my faded denims and my simple tee- shirt.

Well, maybe I wasn't dressed as classily as these girls were dressed, (I didn't even have a single party dress with me in Mumbai), but when it came to matters of figure, I knew I was way up in class with the best of them.

Some of the dudes these girls were with were blatantly staring at me.

My messed up hair and sweat-stained face must have made me look an exciting sight.

I turned my back to them as Ajay came on line.

"Hi babes", I said. "You'll never guess where I am."

He said that if I knew he couldn't guess, then why was I asking him to guess. Why didn't I tell him straight away where I was?

I excitedly told him that Susan, Sheetal, Meena and me had gone shopping, and then Susan had suggested we visit this pub where I now was.

I told him what an exciting place I found it to be, and asked him to come over since I was missing him.

"I just had a couple of dances with two guys, but I was wishing you were here all the time while I was dancing with them", I said, hoping he'd be happy that I was missing him.

"Two guys? Which two guys?" he immediately snapped. "I thought you said you were with your girlfriends."

"I **am** with my girlfriends, sweets", I told him soothingly. "These are just some guys we met at the pub. I don't even know them. One of them just came up to our table and dragged me on to the dance floor and then - - - - - "

I realised I was speaking to thin air.

Ajay had cut the phone off.

I couldn't believe it.

Was he that jealous?

I called him again, but he didn't pick up.

"Oh well", I said to myself, "I can't spoil the evening for the other girls", and I walked back in to join them, all the while thinking what funny creatures guys were. Ajay could sleep around with an older woman and blatantly tell me about it, and I couldn't even dance with a guy my age for five minutes without him getting upset about it.

I walked back into the pub. The place was now almost bursting with people.

I couldn't see any of my friends, but Meena saw me and pulled me over to join her at our table. "Where **have** you been?" she shouted loudly into my ear, to make herself heard over the music. "Sure you won't have another drink?"

"Might as well", I thought to myself. "Make it a small one", I yelled back in her ear. "After that, I'll really have to leave. I've got to get home by ten. I don't want any hassles in these last few days that I'm staying with aunt."

Then Meena removed a pack of cigarettes from her purse, lit a cigarette for herself and held out the pack towards me, offering me one.

"I didn't know you smoked", I asked her, surprised. Although I knew her as a classmate since a year, I'd never seen her smoking.

"I don't often smoke in public", she said. "Although it's no big thing nowadays. But I always carry a pack in my purse and have a quick smoke in the loo once in a while. It's silly of me, but it's just that I'm a bit old-fashioned that way."

Well, Dear Diary, I'd seen many girls smoking in this city,

even many in my institute, but none of them had ever offered me a puff before. I wasn't too keen on having a drag, but I didn't want to seem stuck-up, so I hesitantly took the cigarette which she lit for me, and inhaled.

I sort of sucked the smoke into my lungs and I burst into a coughing fit.

"Hey, take it easy. You're supposed to just take it in lightly, not try to swallow it", said Meena, banging my back with her fist and handing me a glass of water.

I gradually ceased coughing.

A thought suddenly flashed through my mind.

This is how the thought went, Dear Diary.

I thought that although I'd been in Mumbai for a year, this day was a first for me in so many ways.

There were so many places I hadn't been to and so many things I hadn't done and tried out so far.

Until now, it had been college till evening, a coffee or maybe a movie with friends or with Ajay, shopping, maybe a light snack somewhere and then home for dinner.

I was still a babe-in-the-woods as far as this big city went.

But today, I had three firsts.

My first pub visit.

My first drink.

And my first cigarette.

All this flashed through my mind while in the midst of my coughing fit.

At last, I stopped coughing, and I gasped in smoke filled air.

"I think I better leave", I told Meena in a choked up voice – "I need to get home."

She didn't press me to stay. She knew about my family situation.

She came out with me into the lobby. "Are you sure you're okay?" She looked concerned. "Why don't you call Ajay if he's nearby? He'll be glad to drop you home."

I wished she hadn't reminded me about Ajay.

What **WAS** wrong with him? Every time I felt I was getting closer and closer to him, he managed to act so strange and distance himself away from me.

Anyway, I was more than capable of getting home on my own. My aunt's place was just fifteen minutes away from the pub by rickshaw.

I hugged Meena, thanked her for a terrific experience, told her to say bye to Susan and Sheetal for me, (they were still somewhere on the dance floor), and then stepped out on to the road and caught an auto-rickshaw.

The traffic on the way home was pretty bad. It was now around eight-thirty in the evening, and that's the time when most people in Mumbai are on their way home from work.

It didn't take me the fifteen minutes to reach home that I'd expected it would take. It was closer to forty five minutes. The rickshaw crawled along in the traffic at a snail's pace.

By now, the two drinks I'd had and the smoke I'd inhaled were starting to hit me and my head was reeling. I noticed the rickshaw driver staring at me through the rear view mirror, and I immediately made an extra effort to sit erect and look in full control of my senses.

I didn't want him getting any wrong ideas.

The rickshaw at last reached the road which led to my aunt's building. By now it was nine fifteen. I paid the driver off and steadied myself, and walked up to the second floor apartment which was still to be my home for a few more days.

I took a deep breath and rang the bell. My aunt opened the door and sniffed, obviously smelling the smoke which clung to my clothes and maybe getting the stink of gin on my breath. (I should have had the sense to pop a mint into my mouth before coming home, but I'd hardly thought of it at that time.)

Well, for a few seconds, my aunt didn't say a word. Words failed her.

Then she hissed in a low tone – "Just get straight into your room and stay there. You're simply **stinking** of tobacco and alcohol. My daughter's in the living room and I don't want you even going near her."

I mumbled an apology and walked to my room, entered, and silently closed the bedroom door.

I could make out from my aunt's tone that I wasn't going to get any dinner.

I only regretted that I hadn't had a bite to eat while I was at the pub.

This whole drink business suddenly didn't seem all that great to me. Give me good solid food over a drink any day.

Hunger pangs were gnawing at me, but I could control them for one night. After all, I knew I had only myself to blame. Looking at it from my aunt's perspective, putting myself in her shoes, I guess I would have reacted the same way that she had done.

After all, her daughter was really a good kid, and although I wasn't a bad person myself (I've never intended harm for anyone in my life – and that's **my** definition of a 'good person'), I had to admit I wasn't exactly setting a good example or being a great role model for a impressionable young school-girl whose parents had great expectations of her going far in life.

I changed into my nightie, peeped out my room, saw no one outside in the corridor, and stepped quietly to the loo and then to the wash-basin to brush my teeth. I simply **had** to gargle out the taste of gin from my mouth and then wash out the smoke from my face, else I'd never get any sleep that night.

Feeling better, I quietly walked back to my room.

I didn't feel like reading, but I didn't feel sleepy either. I just switched off the lights, kept a small night-lamp on to give me company, and lay down in bed.

My mind kept thinking all sorts of vague thoughts. It kept darting all across the world.

My thoughts kept shifting from mummy and papa and *dadi* to Ajay.

Shifting from Dehradun to Mumbai and back.

I wondered how beautiful it would be if we human-beings could just physically flow with our thoughts, and reach the place we wanted to reach by just thinking about it.

But then I immediately realised that if that were possible, no one would need aeroplanes or air-hostesses either for that matter.

I would be out of a job before I'd even begun.

I laughed at the silly way my thoughts were flowing.

By now, the effect of the gin was wearing off.

I wondered casually how some people seemed to swallow whole bottles of the stuff and not have it affect them. Two pegs had been enough to make my head spin for a couple of hours. Maybe the first time had this effect on everyone.

Lost in these vague thoughts, I suddenly got a shock.

Fingers were softly running through my hair.

"Preity", came a whisper. "Preity, are you awake?"

It was a female voice.

It was a kind voice.

Was it my cousin Nisha?

No. It didn't sound like her.

Although I couldn't for heaven's sake imagine who other than Nisha could be treating me so kindly in this house.

The fact that it could have been my aunt didn't even cross my mind.

But that's exactly who it was.

I could have sent it as an entry to the 'Ripley's Believe it Or Not' show.

It was that unlikely, but true.

"Yes, I'm awake", I said hesitantly, still not sure that it was my aunt, or whether I was dreaming of receiving the loving gesture I so badly needed.

She kept stroking my hair, and with her other hand, she softly caressed my cheek, while I lay with my head on the pillow.

"Preity, can I talk to you?" she said, in a kind and soft tone.

"Sure", I said. I didn't know what else to say. This sudden twist in her behavior was zapping me.

"You know Preity", she said. "I never went to college. Your mother never went either. Your mother never minded it as she was already in love with your dad from a young age, and only wanted to be his wife as soon as possible.

But **I** minded not attending college.

I minded it terribly.

It was my one dream since my schooldays.

I'd always wanted to study further.

But when I passed out of school, our dad passed away, and I couldn't burden our mom with my college fees and other expenses. So I got a job and helped out the family from a young age.

Then I got married, and my dream of going to college remained just that.

An empty dream."

She paused, and a tear fell on my cheek.

I was shocked.

Aunt? Crying?

She always seemed so tough. As if she could handle everything.

That's when I realised that it's not only us youngsters who put on a mask to face the world.

Everybody does it.

She must be hurting so badly from inside.

But why had she to come and say all this to me? That was what was puzzling me.

Then she went on.

"Well, Preity. Unfortunately, I couldn't live my dream. But I have a daughter. A brilliant daughter. And I want to live my dream through her. It's my last chance. My **only** chance.

When my sister, that is your mom, requested me if you could stay with me for a year while you completed your studies in Mumbai, I couldn't refuse. I owe your mom so much. So much."

She paused again as if to recollect the childhood days.

I had a sudden urge to transport myself back in time and see how my mom and my aunt looked as schoolgirls. Was I like them? I know I look very much like my mom did at this age. But what about as a person? Was I different? Or alike? And would my future be the same as hers?

Wild thoughts, Dear Diary. Wild thoughts.

Then my aunt went on. "But Preity, when your mom told me you were studying to be an air-hostess, I was terrified. Terrified that my Nisha would get carried away with the same idea. Nisha has always been glamour struck. Right from a young age, I've had a tough time getting her to focus on her studies.

She's brilliant, but she's star-struck.

And she's good looking. Like all the women in our family.

I want her to study further and further, and not end up in films or serials or modeling or even to be an air-hostess.

That's why I hardly even let her watch TV. I want her to take up a serious profession.

I know it's wrong on my part, but I can't help it. This dream of mine has remained a dream for too long.

Through Nisha, I want my dream to become a reality. I want her to be what I could never be."

In the dim light of the room, I could see she had her face in her hands, and was heaving, sobbing soundlessly.

I kept lying down on the bed. I felt she'd be embarrassed if I saw her crying.

Then she gained controlled of herself.

"I'm really, really sorry Preity", she said. "Believe me, it's hurt me to treat you this way. Every night I pray and ask for forgiveness because I've been so unkind to you.

But I just didn't want you coming between me and my dream. I'm really not like this. I've put on a mask ever since you've come to stay with us. Believe me, it's been really difficult for me to be so strict and stern with you. You've never seen the real me. But I'll make it up, I promise.

It's just that I couldn't stand seeing you enjoying yourself with your friends, having a nice time, doing what girls your age should be doing, because I felt guilty at preventing my own daughter from doing the same.

Tonight, when I sent you off to your room without dinner, all my bottled-up feelings of the past one year came out. I started to hate myself.

Why was I treating a nice young girl, my own sister's daughter, in this shabby manner?

I know you're young. I know you need friends and company. I also know you're sensible and you know your limits.

Oh, don't ask me how I know. I can tell. I was your age not so long ago, you know?"

There was a smile in her voice now.

I sat up straight and faced her, looking into her eyes.

I'd always thought mom had made a mistake by sending me here to stay where I was not wanted.

Now I know why they say – **Mother really knows best.**

Aunt continued – "Thank you for coming to stay, Preity. You've opened my eyes. I can't change as a person overnight, but I'll definitely be less pushy with Nisha now.

I'll let Nisha listen to her own heart, rather than to mine.

I thank you Preity, and I'm sure Nisha will thank you too.

Your coming here has changed our lives for the better. I'll be able to have a relationship with my daughter that I never had before. Bless you, Preity."

"Oh, I nearly forgot", she said. "I'll get you something to eat. Do you want to come out and have it or should I get it to your room?"

I decided to have it in my room and that's what I told her.

It was so nice to talk to her alone, that I didn't want my uncle or Nisha sharing this moment. Now that I knew what a nice person she was, I selfishly wanted my aunt all to myself for some time.

It felt exactly as if I had my mom here with me.

I liked it.

She was gone for five minutes, and I just lay my head on my pillow and rested.

She returned with some hot *doodhpaak* and *poories*. Yum.

I had a bite, and then gave her a bite as well. Food tastes double good when you share it, Dear Diary.

She swallowed the bite, then cradled my head in her hands.

I wept.

I wept and I prayed.

I prayed she would be able to live her dream through her daughter.

She deserved it.

God, please grant that her dream comes true.

I finished my bowl of *doodhpaak*, wiping it clean with the last *poorie*.

I thanked her for being my mother for this one year, and told her that although I was moving, I would always keep in touch. I needed to learn to be on my own, to be independent, and handle issues myself without a family to always back me up. It was all part of the learning and growing process, and the sooner I did it, the better.

She told me that I was more than welcome to stay here till I'd found a place.

"No time deadlines in the evening now", she laughed. "You can come home as late as you like, and there'll always be hot dinner waiting for you, *beti*."

"*Beti*."

"*Beti*."

This was the first time she'd called me that.

This was the first time anyone had called me that in the last one year, ever since I'd been in this city.

I'd always had a roof over my head.

But today, Dear Diary, in this city of ten million people, I knew I had found a **HOME.**

My eyes went moist.

She said she would come with me on my house-hunt and make sure I was well settled in a good place with good room-mates. And whenever I needed family, she was just a shout away.

She told me to come over often for dinner, as often as I liked. "Though I know as an air-hostess you've got to keep yourself nice and trim", she joked.

I promised her I'd take time out and regularly come over and speak to Nisha about pursuing a good career. Sort of be a good elder sister to her. It was the least I could do.

We chatted some more, then my aunt hugged me, said good-night, and left to join uncle in the living room.

I lay down, zapped at the turn of events.

Pleasantly zapped.

Delightfully zapped, Dear Diary.

Just when you think you've figured out people, they do a hundred and eighty degree U-turn and surprise you.

I knew now that whatever problems I faced in this city, the load would be lightened, because I'd found an anchor to hold on to.

And then I just crashed, Dear Dairy.

I was out like a light.

The first time in a year since I'd been away from home, I had an undisturbed sleep.

Date : 7th June

And so, Dear Diary, that eventful day was a day of many learnings.

Many, many learnings for young Preity Singh.

I learnt, Dear Diary, that people can put on masks for many reasons.

The reasons are many. But the lesson you learn from it is one.

Until you look beyond the mask, there can be no true relationship.

And to look beyond the mask, Dear Diary, requires the viewer to be less selfish. To consider the feelings and emotions and expectations of the one who has put on the mask.

And I learnt, Dear Diary, that when I am involved in a mis – understanding, it is exactly that.

I missed understanding the other person.
Just as the other person may have missed out on understanding me.

And we both miss out on understanding each other because we are so caught up in our own selfish little selves.

The more effort we make to truly listen to the drumbeat of the soul of each other, and understand their rhythm, the smoother our lives will be.

So I will practice the art of listening with my heart, and not just with my ears, Dear Diary, and I will become a better person for doing that.

I learnt, Dear Diary, that every human being, whether he shows it or not, has worries, and it is not just us youngsters who have problems and need support. Grown-ups have problems too.

And most important, Dear Diary, I learnt that I need to improve on my own shortcomings before pointing out the shortcomings of others.

God Bless this day, Dear Diary. It has taught me so much.

Date : 11th June

House Hunting

Dear Diary
The last three days, I've been busy hunting.

Oh, not tigers, or lions, or even deer.

You know I love animals tooooo much. I can't bear to think of any of God's creatures in pain.

No, Dear Diary, my 'hunt' today was of a very different and difficult kind.

I was house-hunting in the city of Mumbai.

Not buying a house, Dear Diary. Mumbai is faaaaar tooooo expensive for me to even think of buying my own house. It's a lovely city, but I do wish that finding accommodation here was not such a mammoth task.

But as an old song goes, let's start at the very beginning, a very good place to start.

So let's start this episode in my life three days ago.

73

Because three days ago, I started the journey of finding a paying-guest accommodation for myself.

I got up nice and early and had a refreshing shower. By the time I finished, Nisha was on her way to school. I hugged her and off she went, schoolbag on her back.

I've really gotten fond of Nisha in this last one year, Dear Diary. I'd hardly ever met her before, what with me spending my life so far away in Dehradun and she being brought up in Mumbai.

And all of a sudden I find I have a cute ready-made, ready to love, younger sister.

I smiled and waved her 'bye' from the balcony as she boarded her school bus.

Then I moved to the dining table where aunt had laid out a special breakfast for me.

There were sizzling hot *aloo-parathas* with curd, and fresh lime juice. Yummmmm.

Aunt has changed so much in the last few hours, that I now feel I have **TWO** moms.

One – my own dear, sweet mom back home in Dehradun. The **bestest** mom in the whole wide world.

And now I had Mom Number Two – a lovely combination of aunt / mom right here in Mumbai.

As uncle had left for work already (in Mumbai, everybody leaves home early and reaches home late in the evening from work, as travelling here consumes a lot of time), me and aunt sat down and demolished all the *aloo-parathas* together.

Aunt laughed at the sight of me attacking the *parathas* with relish. She said, "Preity, don't you know that these *parathas* are full of fattening *desi ghee*? I thought all air hostesses had to watch their figure."

I smiled and replied, "I know, but I'm having so many of them because they're also full of that special and priceless ingredient – **Love.**"

Aunt laughed again and said that this reminded her of an old joke – Where the punch-line goes that if **YOU** don't watch your own figure, no one else is going to watch it either.

She smiled and slyly asked me if the guy who'd dropped me home on the bike a few days back was someone special.

With my mouth full of *paratha* and curd, I just nodded a 'yes'.

I felt so good that I could now share these confidences with her. I was only sad that we had developed such a great rapport just at the moment I had to leave their place and find my own accommodation.

Aunt was coming along with me for the house-hunting expedition. In fact, we had arranged to leave right after breakfast.

She'd warned me that it would not be an easy job.

"You've got a budget to think of. Then the locality and building need to be decent. And I don't want you staying too far away from me either. And I want to see that the other girls you'll be sharing the apartment with are decent girls. I can't have my daughter staying with people I can't trust."

'**My daughter.**'

That felt so, so, soooooo good to hear.

Since I'd finished my breakfast, I got up and hugged her tight.

"Ow, Preity, you're suffocating me. Let **GO**." But she had a huge smile on her face as she said this.

We cleaned up the breakfast plates, got dressed in practical clothing. (Aunt said we could be out all day, exploring apartments and climbing floors in buildings which may have no elevators, so it was best to wear something comfortable.) I wore my trademark jeans and a light coloured tee-shirt. Aunt put on a *salwar-kameez* and tennis-shoes, and we were ready for action.

The first stop we had scheduled was to meet an estate agent who'd been recommended to aunt by a friend of hers. He specialised in providing paying-guest accommodations for working girls in the locality of Andheri. That is where aunt stayed, and that's also near to where the airport in Mumbai is located. So that's the locality I was looking for to stay myself.

It's also a locality which would fit into my budget, which I'd calculated to be a maximum of seven thousand rupees a month for rent. After all, I was now going to be staying on my own, and all the household expenses that until now my parents, and in the last one year my uncle and aunt had taken care of, were now going to be my baby.

Food would be a major expense. Of course I'd have room-mates to share the cost of things like electricity bills, the gas-cylinder and so on, but I'd still have to pay my share. And then I had to send some money home to dad, buy a nice gift for aunt, uncle, and of course for Nisha. And I had to add some savings to my bank-account at the end of every month.

As a hostess starting a job with a domestic airline, my salary with allowances would be somewhere in the range of twenty five thousand rupees a month. I'd really have to juggle the mathematics to stay on the positive side.

No wonder grown-ups look so tense so much of the time. Paying bills can't be much fun.

Well, anyway, off we went to meet the agent at the appointed place. He was waiting and he greeted us with a smile. Then he got straight down to business, asking me how much my budget would be, so he could accordingly show me accommodation which fitted my budget.

When I told him the amount I was prepared to pay, his face fell. "Is that all?" he queried. "I thought air-hostesses earned really well," he added.

"This air-hostess doesn't," I told him firmly. "I've just got the job and I'm flying with a domestic airline, not an international one," I explained.

"Well, that knocks off quite a few places I was planning on showing you," he said. "With the budget you have, you'll have to share a room with another girl."

"That's fine with me ----," I began, before my aunt interrupted and said firmly – "I don't want my daughter staying with just **any** kind of girls. You make sure that the girls she shares the apartment with are decent people."

A day before, I would have lost my cool at this interruption, but today I felt great that I had someone looking after my interests. I didn't say a word.

"Of course, aunty-*ji*," said the agent soothingly. "You don't think I would show just any old place, would you? I also have a reputation to maintain."

"That's fine then", said aunt, and off we went.

To cut a long story short, Dear Diary, it was a wasted day.

I've never put in so much effort into any activity and seen no result at the end of it.

The agent showed us five apartments, three of which we rejected out-right the moment we saw the buildings. Just because I didn't have a very high budget is no reason why I should stay in a filthy place where the concrete compound has heaps of rubbish lying around and dirty old men hang around the stair-case ogling every female climbing up the stairs.

One apartment which my aunt and me **DID** like, we rejected after seeing who my flat-mates would have been.

It was in a nice building with a decent front lawn (greenery is something which is rare to see in Mumbai), and the agent said it was a two bedroom apartment, which was currently occupied by two girls, who were looking for two more room-mates to join them so they could split the costs.

One of the girls was at home, and as soon as she opened the door, I knew that any chances I had of staying there collapsed the moment my aunt got a look at her. She opened the door in an outfit that comprised little more than underwear, and she was extremely comfortable in letting me, my aunt and the estate agent walk into the apartment without putting on any more clothing.

The hall was strewn with various articles of dress lying on the floor. The floor of the hall was also half covered in cigarette ash. It looked like the remains of a volcano. There were beer bottles lying scattered around the place.

The girl invited us to sit, but my aunt took one horrified look and walked out, straight down the stairs and out of the building. I followed her, and the estate agent followed me rather reluctantly. I think he wished we'd stuck around the apartment for some time and had a good look around the place. He seemed fascinated by the girl.

My aunt didn't say a word till we were a little distance away from the building. Then she turned to the agent, and in a harsh tone told him, "If that's your idea of decent flat-mates, you might as well forget showing us any more places." The agent was a little taken aback, and promised that he personally knew the girls staying at the next place he was going to show us, and he could vouch for them. I was a little amused at all this. I was getting a first-hand taste of the sort of life-style some girls living on their own in the city were having.

We first stopped for a little snack at a small restaurant as it was now two o'clock.

Then the agent took us to a real classy building, where he said that three very **decent, homely** girls (he stressed on the words 'decent' and 'homely', directing them to my aunt), were staying. They were working in good companies and were looking for a fourth girl to join them to share the expenses. He said that since one of the girls here worked at a call-centre in the night shift, she would be home right now.

I fell in love with the building at first sight. We reached the fourth floor apartment and it was opened by a sweet looking girl dressed in jeans and sweat-shirt. She recognised the agent, greeted him, and invited us all in. The living room was neat, almost as spic and span as my mom and my aunt kept their own homes. My aunt had a look around the place and I could make out she approved. The agent introduced the girl to us and explained that we'd come to see the apartment for me to stay. "Oh," said the girl. "I wish you'd come about an hour earlier. Another girl **just** came half an hour ago. She loved the place and we promised her that she could join up with us. I'm **so** sorry. Won't you at least have a cold drink? It's so hot outside."

My heart sank. I could see my aunt was looking upset as well.

"Thanks", I replied, "but we'd better leave. We still have a lot of places to see and we ought to get going."

We said 'bye' to the girl and we left. The moment we were out of her hearing range, my aunt blasted the agent. "Couldn't you have got us here first thing in the morning rather than taking us to see all those stupid places and wasting our time? If we'd come here first, we could have fixed it up by now."

I was feeling a bit upset myself, but I told my aunt to cool it.

The agent said he still had a few more places in mind to show us, but I said we'd prefer to wind up house-hunting for the day and continue tomorrow.

The agent went off in a huff. From his point of view, he'd wasted his day as well, and he'd got yelled at by my aunt on top of it. But I guess he was used to it.

"Well, Preity", said my aunt, "what do we do now?"

"Oh, let's take it easy. I guess something will turn up tomorrow", I said with much more confidence than I was feeling from within. House-hunting in Mumbai was turning out to be every bit as hard as people had warned me it would be. Maybe even harder.

Well, tomorrow would be another day.

Me and aunt decided to do a little shopping before we went home. I bought a cute pair of ear-rings for Nisha and then my aunt bought a pair of sun-glasses for me. We had a coffee and a sandwich someplace and then returned home to meet Nisha, who would be on her way back from school.

Nisha reached home just a little after we did, and while she had her Bournvita and me and aunt had our lemon tea, the three of us indulged in girl talk. It felt so nice to really be a part of the family and chat over the dining table. I almost wished I didn't have to leave this place.

But suddenly, during this conversation, there was good news.

From an unexpected source.

Nisha, who was aware about the house-hunting expedition, had excitedly spoken about it to a school-friend of hers. This school-friend had a cousin from out-of-town, who was working with an advertising agency in Mumbai. This cousin was staying with two other girls in an apartment in Andheri, and they were looking for a fourth girl to join them. This news Nisha relayed to us over her Bournvita and sandwiches.

I looked at aunt excitedly. Maybe this could be the break I was looking for.

Aunt seemed happy as well, as she knew the school-friend Nisha was speaking of, and also knew her family very well. She immediately called the friend's mother, not wanting a repeat of the morning's situation, where a slight delay had cost us such a lot.

She first made small talk, while I waited nearby with clenched fists for her to get to the meat of the conversation.

At last she brought up the topic. She made a few "Uh, uhs" and "ah, ahs" before hanging up.

Then she turned to me and said – "She's getting in touch with Anita right away; that's her niece who's looking for the room-mate. She'll just let us know if they've already found a new room-mate or whether they're still looking."

I waited on tenterhooks, unable to bear the agony of not knowing.

In a couple of minutes the call came through. Aunt picked it up. When she put it down, she turned to me with a beaming smile. "It's all right," she said. "The girls would love to meet you as soon as possible. I didn't ask her too many details, but I know the family well, and I'm sure any member of their family would be putting up in a decent place and living in a decent manner. If you like, we can go there today evening around eight to have a look. The place is quite close by, and Anita should be back home from work by then."

Well, the rest of the evening passed in a blur.

I took Nisha to an ice-cream parlour down the road as first installment of her 'treat' as she was the one who'd given me the lead in the house finding.

She had a Swiss Sundae and I had a Praline Cream. What fancy names, Dear Diary. I remember when I was a kid back in Dehradun not so long ago, the only options we had were vanilla and chocolate.

I bought a family-pack of ice-cream which I carried home and presented to aunt so we could all have ice-cream after dinner that night.

At around seven-thirty, me, aunt and Nisha (Nisha was just as excited as I was about the entire process), set off to see what would hopefully be my new home.

It was pretty close by from aunt's place, just about a couple of kilometers away. The building was situated in a nice, quiet neighbourhood, and had a good 'feel' about it. You know I'm like that, Dear Diary, I can sense the good aura of a place even if I see it for the first time. I instinctively knew I'd be happy if I lived here for any length of time.

As we entered the building, I prayed that it would work out. Even finding a job had not been as difficult for me as finding accommodation seemed to be.

Aunt sensed I was nervous about the outcome, and she gripped my hand and looked in my eyes and smiled. At that moment I knew I was going to stay here. My guardian angel had looked at me through my aunt's eyes and assured me of it.

Feeling much calmer now, I waited for the door of the apartment to open.

A cute girl, almost my mirror image in looks and figure (apart from my slightly Chinky features), opened the door.

"Hi, you must be Preity. Hello aunty, how are you? And is that Nisha? Hi, Nisha, nice to meet you. I'm Anita. Come in, come in, come in, and please excuse any mess", and we were welcomed into what was going to be my new home.

I liked Anita instantly. I've never had a best friend since I've come to Mumbai, and I was certain she and I would hit it off.

I liked the room as well. It was neatly furnished. Reasonably well kept. There was hardly any sign of any 'mess'.

Of course, you could hardly expect single working girls to spend too much time on house-hold upkeep.

We sat down and Anita got us some water. "Tea, or something cold?" she asked.

"No thanks", aunt replied. "We've to rush back home. I still have to cook dinner. My husband will be arriving home from work any minute. We just came to settle the accommodation issue for my niece, Preity. She's got a job as an air-hostess, you know," said aunt proudly.

I couldn't believe my ears. Aunt; proud of my being an air-hostess? And saying this in front of her own Nisha? I just couldn't believe it. I loved her even more at that moment.

But then I turned to pay attention to what Anita was saying.

"Sure," said Anita. "Let me explain the set-up here. It's a three bedroom apartment. The owner is a lady. We call her Sharma aunty. She's a widow and has a daughter who's married in Delhi. Sharma aunty spends quite a lot of her time with her daughter over there. Sharma aunty is well-off and really doesn't need the extra money, but when she is in Mumbai, which is about one week in every month, she likes to have some company. So she uses one bedroom herself and lets out the other two bedrooms to four girls. When she's not in town, we girls have the place to ourselves. A few conditions that we have to follow are; no parties to be held here, no loud noise which would disturb the neighbours, no non-veg food to be cooked or eaten in the house (eggs are allowed), no smoking, no drinking (not even beer), and no guys to visit the place after eight in the evening.

It sounds quite a long list, but if you realise, it's really very sensible, and hardly restricts or inconveniences us in any way. We're all given keys to the apartment, and we can come and go any time we please.

Last week, one of the girls staying with us left as she got married. Sharma aunty was here for the marriage. She treats us like her own daughters and she trusts us completely. In fact she's gone back to Delhi, but she's told me if I can find a girl who would like to take up the accommodation, and if I feel the girl would fit in, I could let her take up the vacant place.

The rent's not too high. Sharma aunty has fixed the rate at a flat twenty four thousand rupees a month as a fixed amount. I'm responsible for collecting it from all the girls and handing it over to her. So we each contribute six thousand a month and Sharma aunty takes care of the electricity and water bills and the society charges. It's a decent building with good neighbours and proper security.

I've been staying here for three years. I'm the oldest here. I work as a creative person with an advertising agency. I share one bedroom with Payal, who flies with Air Dubai. If you join us, Preity, you'll be sharing a bedroom with Khushboo, who's a model and acts in serials on TV. She's a really nice girl. You'll love her. So helpful. Normally whenever a girl leaves this place, we get a replacement within a day as the place is so nice. But this time we've all been so busy with Hemal's wedding, (she's the flat-mate who just got married and has left), that we've not really informed anyone that we have a place vacant. It's just that I spoke to my aunt about it yesterday. She must have told my cousin, who's with **YOUR** cousin in school," she smiled at Nisha, "and here we all are."

She paused and smiled at each of us. "Are you **SURE** I can't get you anything, or would you rather see the place first if you're in a hurry to leave?"

My aunt was beaming. This was the kind of girl she liked. Sensible, mature, responsible, trustworthy. I liked her too.

"Let's see the apartment?" I said, looking enquiringly at aunt.

"Yes, let's," she said as she got up. Nisha followed too.

We'd already seen the living room, which was painted a nice pastel colour and had soft lighting, it had a dining table with six chairs, an LCD television, (which Anita said all the girls could use, provided they didn't fight over which channel to watch), two neat sofas and a couple of bean-bags to flop down on. A large window overlooked a garden. All in all it was a lovely, homely room.

We followed Anita and she first took us to the kitchen. It was a neat, well laid-out kitchen. It had an aqua-guard, a gas stove, a microwave and all the necessary pots and pans stacked in proper order.

"We either get ready stuff from outside and heat it up in the microwave, or if one of us is in the mood, we try our hand at cooking," explained Anita. "Me and Payal are just about average in the kitchen, the *daal* and rice types, but Khushboo is a fantastic cook. And so is Sharma aunty of course. She loves to cook for us as well, so we really have no problem about meals when she's in town. How good are **you** at cooking, Preity?" she asked.

"Not too good and not too bad," I grinned and replied. I was beginning to love this place. So warm. So friendly. So much like **HOME**.

Then we moved through the rest of the house. First we came to a locked door. "That's Sharma aunty's room," Anita explained. "She keeps it locked, but leaves the key with me in case there are any emergencies like any wiring problem or some short-circuit or something like that. Her room has an attached bath, whereas for us there's a common bathroom just outside."

Then we reached another bedroom. "This is mine," said Anita. "This is the room I share with Payal." There were two neat beds, two wardrobes, and a large soft-toy on the floor. "That belongs to Payal", she giggled. "She can't bear to part with it." There was a small music system. "We all enjoy music," she said. There was a large window, overlooking the road.

Then we went to what would be **MY** room, Dear Diary.

I fell in love with it at once.

There were two beds here as well. "That bed will be yours", she pointed out to the bed near the window. And this will be your wardrobe." She opened a neat wooden wardrobe, quite spacious.

The room had a lot of posters stuck on the wall. Anita noticed me staring at the posters and explained – "Your room-partner, Khushboo, is a hard-rock fan. She'll travel all the way to Bangalore or Chennai or even Dubai if there's a concert going on. As I told you, she's a model and also acts in serials on television. You may have seen her in this serial, 'Working Girl' where she plays the role of Malini.

"Oh, yes," said aunt. That's one of my favourite serials. And she acts soooo well. Imagine Preity, you'll be sharing a room with a celebrity."

Nisha was the most thrilled of the lot. She was exploring the house as though she were going to be staying here herself.

"I love it", I stated with conviction. "I simply **love** it. I'm soooo glad that the house we saw yesterday never worked out. This place is ten times nicer. And everyone here sounds so friendly and helpful. I feel I've already found a new family."

"Well", said aunt to Anita, "then if it's okay from your end and you have Sharma aunty's permission to select a new flat-mate, and since Preity obviously loves it, **AND** most importantly," she said smiling, "**I approve**, when could she move in?"

"Whenever she likes," said Anita. "Hemal, the girl who's married has gone and she's taken her stuff with her. Her wardrobe's empty, so Preity can get her stuff and move in whenever she likes. It'll be good company for me to have someone around as well. The other two spend so much of their time away from home, that it gets pretty lonely for me. Just let me know when you'd be getting your stuff so one of us can be at home to let you in and help you arrange it. I'll give you a spare key for the front-door for yourself once you've settled in."

"Oh God. Look at the time", said aunt suddenly, looking at her watch. "My husband must be back home from work and waiting for dinner. We better rush back. Preity, just decide when you'd like to get your stuff over and tell Anita. If you can't decide right now, then decide later and give her a call. But we **HAVE** to get going. Bye Anita, thanks so much for everything, and **PLEEEEASE**, take good care of my daughter."

"Don't worry about a thing, aunty. She's in good hands," said Anita, and gave aunt, me and Nisha a tight hug. "She's **OUR** responsibility now."

We left in a rush, waving hands and promising to keep in touch.

At the doorstep, I suddenly remembered that I hadn't given Anita any money as a token amount, and I asked her how much I had to pay her now.

"Oh, relax", she said. "There's no hurry for that. You can get six thousand the next time you come. Bye, and see you soon."

We took a cab and rushed home, chatting excitedly along the way about what a lovely apartment it looked and what a nice girl Anita was. I thanked Nisha from the bottom of my heart. After all, it was through her friend that we came to know about this place. "I owe you a special treat", I told her. "Just tell me where you'd like to go." She said she'd think about it and let me know.

When we reached home, uncle was pacing around the living-room, like a tiger waiting for his dinner. But when we told him the news, he was happy for me. "Tell me which day you'd like to shift, Preity. I'll take a day off from office and we'll take all your stuff in the car and help you shift. We'll all go along, and once you're settled in, we'll all go out for a movie and then for dinner."

My eyes sparkled and brimmed over with tears. Everyone was being so genuinely nice to me, I just couldn't help it.

Nisha jumped with joy. "Dad, let's go to see – 'The Man from Brazil'. I heard it's a super movie. And then let's go for dinner to 'Rasoi'. My friend went there last week and she said the food's terrific."

We all laughed at seeing how excited she was.

Then we paused and all laughed again, just for the joy of the moment.

That's the best type of laughter, Dear Diary, where you laugh for no special reason, but just in sheer happiness at the joy of being alive.

That's what I guess they call the laughter of the soul.

Then aunt went to the kitchen to get dinner ready, and I followed to help her.

Nisha got the table ready, (that was her task at home), and uncle sat to read the evening paper.

We had a light but lovely dinner of tomato soup and *poorie bhaji* and then we played cards till it was time for bed.

Next morning, I woke up early with a happy feeling in my heart. I wanted to savour every moment of these last few days that I was staying with aunt, uncle and Nisha. Although I was already thinking of my **NEW** family with whom I'd soon be staying – Anita, Sharma aunty and the rest of the girls.

We had breakfast together, and then Nisha left for school and uncle left for work. "Let me know when you want to shift, Preity", he reminded me as he left. "I'll have to inform office that I won't be coming to work on that day."

"I'd like to move in the day after tomorrow. That's Friday", I said. I wanted to stay at least one more day with aunt before I moved. And my six weeks of training with the airline would be commencing from Monday. I felt I needed a couple of days to settle in and get a feel of the new place and soak in the surroundings before my training began.

The next day, after me and aunt finished our breakfast, I decided to start packing my stuff. Aunt got me a TV carton and helped me fit in all the stuff I'd got with me from Dehradun as well as all the stuff I'd managed to accumulate in the last one year in Mumbai. Clothes, and shoes, and books and all the other million and one knick-knacks that girls just need to have.

It's so strange, Dear Diary, how we girls manage to shop and increase our possessions without even realising it.

I couldn't let any of it go.

Even if it **was** junk, it was **MY** junk.

As I shut the carton, I suddenly felt a tinge of sadness.

So many questions, so many insecurities, about what the future held for me floated around in my mind. What did the future have in store for me, Preity Singh, small town girl from Dehradun, now going to be flying high, thirty thousand feet above the ground?

Whatever it was – if it was good, I would enjoy it. And the parts which were not so good, I could make better by prayer.

"Preity, are you done with your packing?" That shout from my aunt woke me up from my day-dream.

"Yes, I am", I replied.

"It's time for lunch, come on."

I joined her for lunch with mixed feelings.

Today was the last time I would be having lunch in this home as a family member.

The next time I had lunch here, I would be a guest.

Aunt had prepared a special lunch, winding it up with *shrikhand*, which I just love.

We chatted for a while, and then she hugged me and said,

"Preity, I'm really going to miss you. I wish we'd got to know each other better a lot sooner. But it's all my fault. I know I'm to blame."

I looked up and saw a tear in her eye.

"Don't cry," I said, truly touched. "I've been to blame as well. I was insensitive. I should have realised that I was a role model for Nisha. Don't worry, aunt. Nisha's sure to be a success in life. And just as you've taken care of me, I'm going to take care of her. Forever. I mean it."

"God bless you, Preity, and thanks. I know you will," she said.

The rest of the day passed by in a blur. We'd informed Anita that we'd be moving in the next day sometime early in the morning, so that I could have some time to unpack and set up my stuff with aunt and Nisha there to help me. Anita had said that although she'd be at work, Khushboo, the model and actress with whom I was going to share the room, would be there, as she was back from a shoot and had the day off. This was good news. I'd already met and liked Anita. Now I was going to meet Khushboo, my room-mate. I hoped I would like her too.

The next day I woke up real early. It was a bright and sparkling day.

God had gifted me a lovely day to celebrate entering my new home.

I said a short prayer, then went and had breakfast together with everyone.

Then we all got dressed. I helped uncle carry my carton of stuff down to the car, and Nisha carried my handbag and my purse.

"All ready to start a new life, Preity?" asked uncle, as he started the car and drove out of the building.

"Yes, I am", I said hesitantly, in a soft voice. I'd twisted my neck around and was taking a last glimpse of the apartment where I'd learnt so much and grown so much, all just in the span of one short year.

I suddenly thought with a feeling of sadness about how people who were uprooted from their homes in which their families had lived for generations, felt.

Refugees in exile.

So many people around the world. Simple, home loving people, who wanted nothing more than to live and be left alone in peace.

Even poor birds having to leave a tree where they'd themselves been hatched, then grown up, and also brought up their young, flying away, unable to resist the woodcutter's axe.

Well, I couldn't do anything for any of them, however much I'd have liked to, apart from sympathise and pray. But prayer itself has a lot of power, if it's done with unselfish intent.

We soon reached the building where I'd have my new home, and we got the carton up in the elevator. Right up to the seventh floor. Imagine. I'd never stayed so high up before. Preity Singh was really going high up in life in every way.

Khushboo, my room-mate, had already opened the door to the apartment, having seen us arrive with luggage from her balcony.

My first glimpse of Khushboo was ----- well---------- striking.

A cute little pixie-faced girl, barely five feet tall.

Very charismatic face.

Vibrant and bubbly.

A bundle of raw energy.

She'd dyed her bob-cut hair in a combination of lime green and pink.

In short, she reminded me of the phrase that great things come in small packages.

To tell you the truth, Dear Diary, the moment I saw her I felt slightly overwhelmed.

Aunt later mentioned that she thought she looked stunning. (Aunt said that she recalled seeing Khushboo in a serial on TV in which she'd played the role of a submissive daughter-in-law who gets pushed around by everyone. I couldn't ever imagine this little ball of fire being pushed around by even a giant.)

I felt she was a stunner. The impish smile on her face and the twinkle in her eyes told me she'd be fun to be with. Even if I hadn't known that she was a model and an actress, I'd have immediately said that that was the profession that would suit her the best.

She was so different from Anita in looks and personality, yet so much alike in the good, healthy, positive vibes that I could feel generating from her.

"Hi, you must be Preity. Come in. Need any help? Wow, you look so **GOOD**." All this was said in one breath in a lovely sing-song voice that suited her perfectly.

She showed us to her room.

Sorry, **OUR** room, Dear Diary. I was going to be sharing it with her from now on.

"So you're an air-hostess? Wow. That's like, so **GLAMOROUS**."

I told her I thought that her work as a model and as an actress sounded pretty glamorous too.

While me, aunt, uncle and Nisha unpacked my carton and started stacking my stuff neatly into **MY** wardrobe, Khushboo returned with chilled glasses of cola for all of us, and a chocolate bar for Nisha.

"Take a break, have a Kit-Kat", she sang to Nisha, who was absolutely thrilled at having this beautiful television celebrity paying her so much attention.

We finished unpacking by around one-thirty, and Khushboo invited us into the hall for some sandwiches which she'd prepared.

"Pure veg and cheese", she said. "Although I loooove eating non-veg, I don't eat it in this apartment, even when Sharma aunty is not around. I've promised her I won't, so I won't", she said in a determined tone.

My aunt beamed. This girl was definitely someone who could be trusted.

We sat at the dining table in the living-room and had the sandwiches. Aunt started chatting to Khushboo about the serials she'd seen her in and how she enjoyed watching her on TV. Khushboo was thrilled. "Wow, I never realised I had a fan following," she almost blushed.

We finished the sandwiches and helped Khushboo clear away the plates.

She protested, saying we were guests.

"Hey, **I'm** no guest. This is **MY** home," I told her. That set us all laughing.

By now it was three, and uncle said we better rush for the movie if we didn't want to be late.

We asked Khushboo if she'd like to join us for the movie

and then for dinner. "Come on", I said. "We'd love to have you join us."

She tactfully refused, saying that she was tired after her shoot and just wanted to rest. I guess she realised that although we loved her company, we'd like to be all alone by ourselves as a family on this special day.

Speaking of family, Dear Diary, I just wished that my mom and dad and sister and *dadi* were here with us. That would have made my day complete.

But anyway, I'd be seeing them soon. I'd planned on visiting Dehradun on a short trip once my six weeks of training were over.

Thinking of my family back in Dehradun made me want to call mom. She already knew I was shifting, of course, but I wanted to tell her I'd moved in. I gave mom my new address and my new land-line contact. Then aunt spoke to mom, and lastly I made Khushboo speak to mom, introducing her as my new room-mate.

Then off went the four of us to watch '*The Man from Brazil*' and we were all absorbed in the happenings on the screen till seven.

After that, we went for a short drive and had a super heavy dinner at '*Rasoi*', the nice buffet-restaurant recommended by Nisha that had just opened up in the locality.

After the meal, uncle took us for some special home-made ice-cream at a place his office friends had told him about.

After the ice-cream, they all came to drop me off to my new home. I invited them up, but they told me to go ahead, saying it was too late to come up and disturb my friends.

Anita was home from work by now and opened the door for me. "Hiiiiii. Welcome. Naughty girl. You didn't spend your first evening in your new home with your new family."

Khushboo was there as well. They were both having what looked like a late dinner. "Come, join us."

I would have loved to. It smelt soooo gooooood. But my stomach was almost bursting with all the food I'd stuffed inside me.
I joined them at the table and sat on one of the empty chairs.

"Here", said Khushboo, feeding me a bite of *chapati* and *sabzi* with her hand.

Before I could savour and swallow that tasty mouthful, Anita gave me a spoon-full of tomato soup and said, "Try this, it's not packet soup. It's made at home, from real tomatoes."

So with a mixed mouth-full of soup, *sabzi* and *chapati*, and tears of joy flowing from my eyes at having found this wonderful new family, I thanked God for having given me what so many people are still thirsting for – a home.

Date : 14th June

So Dear Diary,
The house-hunting experience has been quite
profound in its own way for me. Apart from
finding out just how difficult getting the right
house is, I also learned so much about life.

I've now decided not to worry too much if I don't get
what I want at first. I'm sure that something better
is waiting around the corner.

I've learnt that people who may appear very
glamorous at first glance may actually have very
kind and loving and helpful hearts hidden just
beneath their painted exterior.

And when it comes to house-hunting or any such
activity, I've concluded that dealing with paid
agents is fine, but it's word-of-mouth from friends
which actually works wonders.

And, Dear Diary, it is important to have a house to
live in, but at the end of the day, nothing can beat
having a home to love in.

Date : 16th August

Airline Training

Well Dear Diary,

It's been a hectic couple of months. Time has just whizzed past. Was on training, you know.

Although our one year aviation course prepared us for most of the things we'd need to know as cabin-crew, each airline conducts its own rigorous training for the staff they select.

Let me tell you about my training with my airline, Dear Diary, I'm sure you'll find it interesting. The entire training lasted for six weeks, and we covered various modules during that period.

Well, to start off, there's the training we were provided on how to serve the customer better. This includes handling various kinds of customer situations and requests, some of which I can tell you are pretty weird.

But then, they are our passengers, and they're entitled to their whims. Don't we all have our own whims, Dear Diary?

Then of course there's the training we're given on grooming, how to wear the skirt and blouse in just the right way, how to tie the scarf in the proper manner, how we should do up our hair, the correct shade of lipstick and eye-shadow and so on. It makes proper ladies and gentlemen out of us.

Another important part of our training was the first-aid training. Absolutely ANYTHING can happen up in the air, right from a lady delivering a baby, to cases of food poisoning, to a person suffering a choking fit. And with every flight not having a doctor on board, it is upon **US** cabin-crew to ensure that we provide immediate first-aid to the passenger till the flight can land. We're trained how to handle cases of burns, choking, and even heart attacks. The medical training we're given is both theoretical as well as practical and follows the Red Cross model. I feel I'm almost a doctor by now, Dear Diary.

Oh, and then of course there's the food service training.

What's a flight without food, right, Dear Diary? What's **LIFE** without food, in fact. So we're given training on how to serve breakfast, lunch and dinner, depending on the time of the day of the flight.

We're shown how the food-tray should be set up for various meals. We're taught the difference between service in the First Class (where soup is served with each meal), and the Business Class (where there's normally no soup, but a starter is provided), and the Economy Class meal (no soup or starter). There are more choices available in the First Class meal, the menu almost resembling an *a la carte* one that you see in a restaurant. Yes, we reaaaaaly pamper our First Class passengers, but that's only fair, since they're paying a pretty hefty price for their tickets.

And after the food-service training is done, we are trained in how to make in-flight announcements, all in polished tones. We're trained to perfect our diction, tone and volume. We have to be ab-so-lute-ly prim and proper while making these announcements. Imagine, Dear Diary, me, Preity Singh, addressing over a couple of hundred passengers all at once, and they all **have** to listen to what I'm saying. It makes me feel like I've sort of moved up in life. (Just kidding, Dear Diary. You know I'll always remain down-to-earth, even if I'm thirty thousand feet up in the sky.)

Then there's the **MOST** important training of all. And that's for **SAFETY**. You know it's strange, Dear Diary, that people tend to think that an air-hostess' job is all about looking glamorous and serving food and drink and doing very little else. Yes, we **DO** spend quite a lot of time in the air serving our passengers, but our **PRIMARY** job is, and will always remain – Passenger Safety. **THAT** is one thing that will always take priority over and above everything else.

This was one of the things taught to me during my aviation course. I was told it could be asked in my job interview as well. And it **was** asked. And fortunately I'd paid attention in class and proudly gave the correct answer.

The question asked to me in my interview was – What is the main purpose of the cabin-crew being on board the airline? The answer – To ensure the safety and security of the passengers on board the flight.

During our safety training, we're shown the various safety equipments such as Oxygen bottles or cylinders, as well as various kinds of fire-fighting equipment. We're also taught how to use them in case of emergencies.

We're explained the procedures to be followed in case of fire, and in case of the aircraft ditching and crash-landing. (I pray it never happens to me Dear Diary. I pray it never happens to **ANYONE.**) But it's always good to be well prepared.

So these are the different kinds of training I went through once I joined the airline. As I mentioned, the training was intensive and rigorous and lasted for a period of six weeks.

And once the training was over – came – **MY VERY FIRST FLIGHT.**

Of course, I wasn't allowed to serve any passengers or make any announcements on my first flight. It's what is called as a **FAMILIARISATION FLIGHT**. After the training period is complete, each of us crew has to undergo three such familiarisation flights, where we are supposed to observe the seniors serving and assisting passengers and see how they go about their job. Just to get us used to the on-board environment. Still, it's exciting to see everything in action. All the training we've received is actually being put into practice by these seniors and we're there to observe and absorb it all.

My first familiarisation flight was from Mumbai to Udaipur, Dear Diary. It was an afternoon flight and it went off smoothly. I had a lovely set of crew flying with me which made it all the better. They really took care of me like a baby. The memory of my first flight as an air-hostess is something I'll always cherish and remember.

And once the three familiarisation flights are over, and we've observed and learnt all that we're supposed to, there are two or three **CHECK FLIGHTS** (also called as Route Checks), that we have to undergo. During these flights we trainee cabin-crew serve the guests their meals as well as tea and coffee, but the senior crew-member on board is closely observing our performance and will submit an appraisal of our performance to the management. These are tense moments, for if things go wrong, it could mean that we don't make the grade as cabin-crew. Fortunately, both of my check flights went off comfortably, (one was a breakfast flight, and during the other flight, we served lunch.) All the passengers I served were sweet and polite. I think my prayers worked.

Whew. Dear Diary. So that completed my training and my check flights.

Now for the **big day.**

What big day?

Oh, I forgot to mention that once we successfully complete our check flights, we get to participate in the **WING CEREMONY.**

The 'Wing Ceremony' is where we are awarded wings which we will now wear on our uniform to indicate that we are full-fledged cabin-crew. We cabin-crew wear half-wings, and the pilots and cockpit-crew wear full-wings on their uniforms. The wing ceremony for my batch was held in a small hotel near our airline office. Fourteen of us from my batch were awarded our wings in that ceremony, which were pinned on our uniforms by a Director of our airline.

I felt sooooo proud Dear Diary, like a soldier being awarded with a medal in battle. The Director pinned the wings above my name-badge on the uniform and wished me a long and happy career ahead. I almost had tears of joy streaming down my face.

After the ceremony, all of us in our batch hugged each other, knowing that we'd never be assembled together in the same room ever again (life takes each of us down strange and different pathways), but for **THIS** moment, **THIS** evening, we were all one and we were on top of the world.

Snacks were passed around, music played and we were at the threshold of a career that many aspire to, but not everyone achieves.

That's that, Dear Diary. About my training, my familiarisation flights, my check flights and my wing ceremony which made me a full-fledged air-hostess.

Date : 19th August

So Dear Diary,
I learnt that whatever one does in life, proper training makes one better at what he or she is doing.

I learnt that even in what appears to be a simple job, there are many elements and skills that need to be mastered to achieve success.

And above all, I learnt that neither sad nor joyous moments last forever. Learn from the sad ones (they always teach you something), and enjoy the joyous moments while they last.

Date : 7th November

Airline Party

Dear Diary
Paaaaarty-time.

Yaaaaaaay.

The word 'Party' reeeeeeeeally brightens up my day.

It's one of my most fav-our-it-est words.

Which are the other words that lift me up?

Gossip.
  Shopping.
Picnic.
  Sunshine.
Birthday.
  Pay-day.
Vacation

What a lovely set of words, Dear Diary.

Sometimes I wish I'd been in charge when language was being developed and words were being created.

I'd have made sure that only such nice, cheerful, bright, glowing words had been invented and no dull sounding ones.

Then everyone would just have to be happy all the time.

But getting back to the party, Dear Diary. (When **WILL** I ever get over this habit of starting a topic and then going off on a tangent.)

I've always **loved** attending parties as well as organising them.

Back home in Doon, it was such a different atmosphere compared to this gigantic city. In Dehradun, almost everybody knew everybody else.

We were all just like one big happy family.

And people there had so much more time for each other. So much more time to get-together and celebrate their birthdays and other occasions.

Ever since my schooldays, I remember attending at least one party a week back home.

In Dehradun, we don't have tall buildings like how they have in Mumbai and other cities. Most of us have our own separate cottages, with a garden in the front and at the back.

In summer, the parties used to be held out in the gardens. The trees were decorated and lit up. The scent of fresh flowers was always in the air. The air itself was clean and pollution free. Unlike in big cities, where people actually pay to go into an Oxygen Bar and breathe pure air for fifteen minutes at a time. If you told someone back home in Dehradun about these Oxygen Bars, they'd say you were crazy.

But then fifty years ago if you'd told a Mumbai local person that his grandchildren would be paying for oxygen, they'd have thought you were crazy as well.

Times change, Dear Diary. And unfortunately not always for the better.

I just hope my Dehradun remains exactly as it is, even a thousand years from now. A sea of calm in an ocean of madness.

As they say, you never value what you have until you lose it.

Sorry, Dear Diary, I'm diverting again.

Anyway, as I was saying, in winters in Dharadun, the parties were held inside our cozy little cottages with plenty of hot 'pahadi' snacks, fresh fruit juices, and home-made birthday cake.

I miss those days.

They are gone, never to return.

Oh, yes, I may go back to Dehradun.

But I can't turn back the clock.

That's why the song I love most is *'Bachpan ke din.'* And Noor Jehan sings it so beautifully.

Sometimes I play that song over and over again on my I-pod. That's the only way I can transport myself back into the by-lanes of past days in Dehradun. God, I sound so old.

But it's such a lovely song.

And such lovely lyrics.

Such a haunting melody.

And sung so well. Straight from the heart.

I may be a girl of the twenty-first century, Dear Diary, but as far as taste in music goes, I also like the melodies of the 1940's and the 1950's.

We never get to hear of such singers and music composers and song writers nowadays.

The other day I overheard a couple of elderly gentlemen discussing the songs and singers of yester-year on my flight. (Yes, Dear Diary, I've finished my training with the airline and been flying since the last three months. As I told you, I've been awarded my **'wings'** at the 'Wing ceremony', which is the aviation term for saying that one has completed one's training and is 'fit to fly'.)

Well, these gentlemen were discussing that these singers with golden voices; Rafi, Mukesh and the rest, were not gone forever. They were merely resting their voices in heaven before taking another earthly plunge. I hope to God they're right.

Sooooo sorry, Dear Diary. You **MUST** stop me when I go off track. I promise I won't do it again. At least not today.

Anyway, speaking of parties, ever since I've been in Mumbai, I haven't attended a **single** party, Dear Diary.

At the most, if it's someone's birthday, the person just takes us friends out for a movie or to a restaurant for lunch or for dinner. And although these lunches are expensive, Dear Diary, it's just not the same feeling as being at a real party.

In the first place, you're sharing the restaurant with so many strangers; and secondly, you just have to sit in one place next to the same person throughout the meal. You can't move around as we did in parties back home.

Or, it's a party organised in someone's tiny flat, where the cramped space makes five people seem like a crowd. It's very rare that people have cottages with front gardens and backyards here in Mumbai.

That's why I was so excited when I got an invite for my first real big party in Mumbai, Dear Diary.

Well, it wasn't a **BIRTHDAY** party, so there wouldn't be any birthday cake, (which is something I just love.)

No other cake ever tastes the same as a birthday cake does. Birthday cakes are sort of magical.

Birthday cakes are so --- so---- they're so **SPECIAL.** Maybe it's because you can't just have them on **ANY** day. It **HAS** to be somebody's birthday.

Well, it wasn't an invite to a birthday party. But, Dear Diary, it was an **AIRLINE** party.

MY airline party.

All airlines host parties once every few months for all their ground and flying staff.

And this was the first time since I'd joined my airline, (it's been around four months now, including six weeks of training), that my airline was hosting a party for us.

My senior friends in the airline told me that at the times when the airline wasn't doing too well financially, then such parties were hosted in a four-star hotel, but now since our airline was doing well, flights were going packed, so this time the party would be hosted in a five-star hotel.

It was to be held on the twenty-ninth of October at the Plaza Deluxe Hotel.

The first thing I did on hearing this exciting news was to check my flight duty-roster.

A roster in an airline is basically a duty chart prepared weekly or fortnightly, which tells the crew which flights they'll be flying throughout that week or fortnight. It lets the crew know in advance what days and what times they'll be on duty so that they can schedule their free time accordingly. If you're not actually rostered to fly on a flight, you could possibly also be on 'stand-by', which means if a crew who is scheduled to fly on that flight calls in sick at the last moment, the person on 'stand-by' would have to take his place. So different crew are on-duty and off-duty at different times, as **SOMEBODY** has to man the flights all the time. Obviously, the ones who're on duty on some flight or the other at the time the party is to be held would miss the party.

I crossed my fingers and just hoped I wasn't rostered to fly or scheduled for 'stand-by' duty on the evening of the party.

With a prayer on my lips, I peeped at my roster.

Yippeeeee.

I **WASN'T** on duty that evening.

I wasn't even on stand-by.

I could attend the party.

And what's more, we'd been told we could get a guest along.

I just hoped that Ajay wouldn't be flying that evening as well.

Of late, me and Ajay hadn't been seeing each other as often as I'd have liked, what with both of us working for different airlines and both of us having busy schedules.

And recently, when we **HAD** been meeting up once a week or so, the evening almost always seemed to end with some silly quarrel over some small issue or the other.

Even the last time we'd met, over ten days ago, we'd ending up arguing hotly about something petty. We'd hardly spoken to each other since then.

I guess all couples go through this phase, Dear Diary. At least that's how I consoled myself.

But I somehow hoped that being at this party together, dancing close with him, would help me get back the Ajay I once knew and had fallen in love with.

I knew Ajay was not on flight right at this moment, so I immediately called him and asked him if he'd be free on the evening of the twenty-ninth.

"Why?" was his blunt response.

"Because I'm inviting you to be **MY** escort to **MY** airline party that evening", I said, feeling rather grand.

He didn't seem too excited at hearing that bit of news.

I know what the problem is with him, Dear Diary, so I really can't blame him. The petty issues we fight over are just an excuse. The real problem is something else.

It's just too bad that it's happened to a lovely guy like him.

He tries to keep it hidden, and not many people know about it.

But of course I'll tell **YOU**, Dear Diary. I can't hide anything from you, can I?

The problem is, that flying really doesn't suit Ajay.

He gets air-sick. It's a medical condition he's afflicted with.

Flying just doesn't physically suit some people.

Like me, he'd rarely flown before he took up the cabin-crew job, so he wasn't aware that flying would affect him this way.

He's mentioned it to me more than once, and it's worrying him a lot.

He tends to feel air-sick and dizzy whenever there's the slightest turbulence in the air. 'Turbulence' is when the aircraft shakes like a jelly due to weather conditions.

He tries to control it and avoids letting the rest of his crew know about it, but you can't keep something like that hidden for any length of time.

It makes him nervous just thinking of getting on board a plane.

If it gets worse, it could mean the end of his flying career, and that's what is making him really irritable nowadays.

I really, really feel sorry for him.

It's just too bad that he gets air-sick.

Every profession has its own unique demands, which would hardly matter in any other profession. Like a model could never go on with her career if she got a scar on her face, or a cook would have to give up his job if his body couldn't stand excess heat. In other jobs, these things wouldn't matter.

It's the same way with a cabin-crew and air-sickness.

Sometimes, life plays cruel tricks.

It gives you everything that you could ever hope for, things that others would die to have, and then it takes away from you some little thing which brings your world crashing down.

Take Ajay for example. He's got the perfect personality for a cabin-crew.

He's handsome.

He's smart.

He's confident.

He speaks so well.

But his air-sickness could cost him his job and his career.

As I said, Dear Diary, if he were in any other profession, this just wouldn't matter.

But as a cabin-crew, where he's got to be flying four or five days a week, being alert all the time and serving people while he's flying, air-sickness is a killer.

And it's this which is shattering his confidence in every area of life.

It's making him so irritable.

It's damaging his relationships with people around him.

It's damaging his relationship with **ME.**

Before this air-sickness hit him, he had always been the

centre of attention, wherever he went.

He always felt he was sort of invincible.

A Superman.

Now he realises he's not perfect.

That he has a weakness.

Now he realises he's only human.

And he doesn't like it.

I really feel so sad.

He's sort of lost interest in life.

He's even stopped shaving on the days he's not on duty.

And he was always so particular about his appearance.

Now, it's almost as if he just ---- doesn't ------ care.

Of course, he still does his job as well as he can, when he isn't feeling air-sick. He's too much of a professional to mess that up.

But after duty hours ------? Well, that's another story.

I've even gone with him to a specialist doctor who's giving him a course of treatment to cure his air-sickness. I just hope it works out. The doctor says the treatment just may work, (or may not), but even if it does, it will take time.

Knowing all this, I try to be as patient as I can with him, Dear Diary, but after all I'm only human. And I have my own job to do and my own apartment to maintain and my own family back home to think of as well. It's not that I don't have any stress in my life.

So beyond being patient with him, Dear Diary, what else can I do? If I **could** do something, I would.

All these thoughts went through my mind while I waited patiently for Ajay to check his own duty-roster.

After what seemed to be ages, he came back on line and told me he was free that evening and that he'd make it for the party.

I was **SO** glad, Dear Diary. I felt **SO** happy.

We made some more small talk and then we hung up.

Our schedules were so packed with flights that the next time we'd see each other would only be on the day of the party.

Then a thought flashed in my mind.

The party was just a few days away.

And I didn't have a **SINGLE** party dress that I could wear.

I hadn't **GOT** any party dresses with me in Mumbai.

My entire wardrobe consisted of my flying uniforms, casual and semi-formal outfits and a couple of formal outfits that I'd worn for interviews when I was job hunting a few months ago.

I panicked.

I simply **HAD** to look my best at the party.

Not that I'm vain, Dear Diary, although every girl **WOULD** like to look her best at a party.

No, it wasn't that.

The reason I was so particular about my appearance at this party was that I wanted Ajay to be reeeeeeeally proud that he was accompanying me.

Although there were many beautiful girls on ground-duty as well as flying for our airline, most of whom would be dressed at their best at the party, I wanted to stand out head and shoulders above them all on that evening.

I wanted every single eye that evening at the party to be on me.

It was one opportunity I thought I was being given to bring back Ajay's interest in life in general and in me in particular.

Maybe he'd revive his interest in life and come out of his semi-depressive state if he realised he's got the most beautiful girl in the entire airline.

That's why my outfit and appearance on that evening was so important to me, Dear Diary.

So I had to answer the following questions, and answer them fast. Reeeeeal fast.

Like – What would I wear?

    – What shoes should I have on?

    – What make-up and hair-do would bring out the best in me?

I decided to tackle these questions in a logical sequence.

First and foremost – The Dress.

I decided I needed help.

Khushboo wasn't home, but since it was a Saturday, Anita was around. Good. I needed her.

"ANITAAAAA", I yelled.

Anita came running from her room, almost tripping over Payal's giant teddy-bear lying on the floor in her hurry.

"What's wrong, Preity? Have you hurt yourself?"

I laughed.

"No, babes, I just need your help to decide on a dress for the office party. You attend so many corporate parties that I feel there's no one better than you to advise me."

She glared at me. "For this you yell and nearly make me break my neck? Preity Singh, you've got some nerve."

"Awww, come on Anita. It's reeeeally important to me. I want to look my best. And who better than you when it comes to fashion advice?" I said, looking at her with pleading eyes.

"All right. All right. Cut the flattery. Let's get down to business. Let's see what you currently have in your wardrobe as of now," she said, all business-like all of a sudden.

I pouted. "I've got nothing except my uniforms, jeans, Tee-shirts, and a formal outfit I wore for my job interview."

She looked zapped. "Preity, you mean to say you've been living in Mumbai for over a year and you don't have a single party outfit with you?"

"Don't rub it in", I said. "I haven't needed one until now. But now I **do**. Where should we go to buy one? You know the best boutiques around."

"How much would you like to spend?" was her first question, and it was a valid one.

"Hmmmm, something upto two thousand bucks?" I said, waiting to see her reaction.

She screwed up her face and thought. "That's not too much, but it's still okay. Then what about shoes, and hair-do. How much are you keeping aside for that?"

My face fell. I'd forgotten that I'd need matching shoes, and I'd need a good hair-do to match my party dress as well, if I wanted to create a killer impact on Ajay.

Anita saw my face and her tender heart melted. "Hey babes, chill. You've got the Fashion Doctor with you, so why worry? I'm taking it up as a challenge that you're going to be the best turned-out chick at the party. You'll make **EVERY** head turn, and **that's** a promise. It won't be too difficult as the raw material I'm going to work on is already beautiful."

I blushed. "There **ARE** going to be many other good looking girls at the party. It's an airline party, you know", I said, trying to sound modest, but secretly delighted with Anita's honest appraisal of my looks.

"Shut up and stop being so modest," frowned Anita. "I'm trying to think what'll look best on you." She had a look on her face which I guess professional designers have when they're faced with a challenge of doing up a model in the best possible manner. I started to feel a little nervous. So much was riding on my looking my best that night.

Suddenly I was shaken out of my thoughts as Anita yelled, "I've got it."

"What, what," I was eager to know. "What kind of dress do you think I can get for two thousand bucks?"

"We're about the same build, aren't we?" she said, examining me critically.

I'd never given the matter much thought, but now that she mentioned it, I guess we were.

"Yeah, so?" I queried.

"So, you dumbo", she said, "why do you want to go out and **buy** an expensive dress in a hurry when you could wear one of mine. And a pair of my matching shoes as well. Then you could spend the entire two thousand bucks on your hair-do and your make-over. Oh, I'm a genius. I love myself," she said, hugging me hard.

I thought it over.

It seemed like a fan-tas-tic idea.

As I'd mentioned, Anita regularly attends the cream of functions as she's into advertising, and apart from having a great dressing sense, she's got a super collection of party dresses and shoes.

"Let's see what'll suit you the best from what I've got. Do you have any suggestions, babes?" she asked me.

"I'll leave it to you. You're the boss girl on the fashion scene", I replied.

She looked pleased.

"Okay. Follow me", she said.

We went to her bedroom.

She opened her wardrobe.

It was like Ali Baba's treasure chest. I'd never seen such a stunning collection of outfits in a single wardrobe before. She rummaged through her stuff, as if certain in her mind what she was looking for. She found it and pulled it out. "There", she said triumphantly. "You'll knock them all dead in this outfit."

I waited curiously to see what she was unfolding.

It was a daring little black spaghetti strap dress. Real skimpy. I recalled seeing her dressed up in it once when she'd gone for a party. I remembered admiring her in it and at the same time wondering when I'd ever have the guts to wear anything so daring and so bold in public.

"And now the shoes", she said, and from the bottom of her wardrobe, she removed a shining black pair of high-heeled stilettos that simply took my breath away. I just **hoped** they'd fit me.

"And here, these will round up the outfit", and she handed me a pair of long sparkling chandelier earrings.

"Anita, you're a magician, and I love you," I said.

"Not so fast", she said. "Let's first see how it all fits on you, or we could try something else."

I prayed it would fit. It all looked so gorgeous. I was sure Ajay would never be able to resist me in this get-up.

I slipped off my Tee-shirt and jeans and put on the dress. It fitted as if it were made for me. Then I tried on the shoes. They were just a leeeeetle bit tight, but they looked mind-blowing. And as I wasn't planning on running a marathon in them, they'd do just fine.

Anita looked at me, pleased with the overall effect.

"It looks great", she said.

"It **FEELS** great", I replied, thrilled.

"Now you'll need a really super hair-do to complement this outfit", said Anita. "I'll take an appointment with you at '*The Spanish Caravan*'. It's a fantastic parlour. I always get a make-over done there if I'm attending any important function. It's a leeeeetle bit expensive, but they'll give you a fantastic total make-over. And you have two thousand bucks to blow. If you need some extra cash, I could lend you some", she added. Anita is always loaded, and she's got a big heart to match her stuffed wallet.

"No babes", I said. ""Thanks, but you've done more than enough for me. I'll manage just fine with the cash I've got."

She called the parlour and took an appointment for the day of the party with a guy named Cherie.

"Sounds like a girl to me", I told her.

"He's the best. Don't argue. Just be there at two. He's busy but I've forced him to squeeze you into his schedule. And now if you really feel grateful to me, Preity Singh, I could do with a nice hot cup of coffee."

I laughed. "Sure Anita, that's a small price to pay for all you've done."

"**I'll** decide the price for my services," she said. "And a cup of coffee prepared and served by an air-hostess doesn't come cheap either."

I giggled, and went off to the kitchen.

On the day of the party, I reached the parlour a little before two and asked for Cherie.

"Yes, dear. Soooo glad you're on time. I haaaate people who're late for their appointments", said a pansyish guy in a girlish sounding voice. I stifled a laugh.

"Thanks for squeezing me into your schedule. I'm due at a party this evening, and I want to look my best", I told him. "Anything special you had in mind, dear?" he asked me.

"I leave it you. I'm wearing a black spaghetti dress with black stilettos, if that's any help", I added.

He glanced at my face from all directions, looked me up and down, then seemed to make up his mind.

He started work by running a generous amount of serum into my long tresses and then proceeded to set it poker straight with tongs. After about half an hour, he loosely put a clip in my hair and started working on my face by putting a matte base on my oily (*Pahadi*) skin. He did up my eyes very bright and sparkly, using a lot of silver, and finished with a coat of black mascara. Finally touching up my lips with a gloss finish, he pulled out the clip and my silky straight hair moulded my face like a beautiful dark cloak.

I looked up into the mirror and just couldn't stop staring and smiling at the beautiful reflection I saw. If I were a guy, I'm sure I wouldn't be able to keep my hands off the beautiful image I saw in the mirror.

"Happy, dear?" he asked, pleased at the expression on my face.

"Not just happy, Cherie, I'm **delighted.** You're a genius. How much do I owe you?"

He mentioned a reasonable figure, and I gladly paid him and gave him a generous tip.

"Have a lovely time at the party tonight", he said, and waved me on my way.

I left the parlour, thrilled with myself, and took a cab home.

Anita was home early from work, working on her laptop, finishing one of her never ending presentations for her clients.

She whistled when I walked in.

"Woooow, babes, is that you? I just couldn't recognise you. Be careful you carry some man-repellant with you when you go to the party. You won't be able to keep the guys off", she raved.

"You're just putting me on", I laughed, but in my heart, I was over the moon.

If **SHE** felt I looked good, it **must** be a genuine compliment.

I gently eased myself onto the sofa, (careful to keep my hair-do intact), read the newspaper, watched some TV and gossiped with Anita till around five-thirty.

At six, I changed into the black spaghetti strap dress, put on my shoes, and sprayed some perfume which was advertised as making the wearer irresistible to men. I sprayed on a little more than I should have, but I couldn't help that now.

I stared into the mirror, not believing the finished effect. Even though I say it myself, it was just ----- too ------ good.

The dress showed a leeeeetle more skin than I'd have preferred, both from the top as well as from below, but I didn't mind. As long as it would make Ajay happy, that was all that mattered.

I went into the living room to wait for Ajay. Anita was in the living room and looked me over appreciatively.

"Wow, babes. You look reeeeally terrrr-iffffic. I wouldn't mind escorting you to the party myself."

I grinned, still slightly nervous about how the evening would go for me.

By now it was almost six-thirty, and I'd told Ajay to pick me up around six-fifteen. I'd planned to spend some quality time before the party alone with Ajay in the hotel coffee shop, and wanted to have a chat with him about where we were heading as a couple.

Six-forty and still no Ajay.

I was just short of biting my nails.

Then the doorbell rang.

I rushed to the door, almost knocking Anita off her feet in my hurry.

"Hey, relax. Take it easy, what's the hurry? Don't be so desperate. Let him wait, he's made you wait long enough", said an annoyed Anita.

I knew she was right, but this wasn't about right and wrong. It was about a guy I loved.

I opened the door.

There he stood.

Handsome as ever.

"Hi, come on in", I greeted him. "You're late", I added, as he walked in.

He greeted Anita, then sat down.

'Yeah, I know I'm late", he said. "I almost wasn't coming. Something urgent cropped up. Then I thought you'd be disappointed, so at the last minute I changed my mind and turned up."

I was so glad he was here, I didn't have the heart to ask him why he hadn't wanted to turn up.

Anita got him a cola from the kitchen. He sipped it slowly, and in the meanwhile all three of us made small talk. At seven, I told him that we really must be getting going. "The venue is at least half an hour away, and the party starts at seven-thirty. I don't want to be late. It's the first airline party I'll be going to", I said.

I hugged Anita, and she wished me all the best. She knew how important this evening was for me. I don't hide anything from her. We're mates, after all.

We left the apartment. Ajay hailed a cab, gave the cabbie the directions, and we got in.

I snuggled up to Ajay in the back-seat, letting him get a whiff of my 'irresistible' perfume.

It was good that the taxi driver knew the way to the hotel, because neither me nor Ajay had our eyes on the road throughout the journey. We'd met each other after so long, and we were sort of making up for lost time.

I felt the evening was off to a great start. I'd managed to get Ajay's attention. Now if only the rest of the evening went as planned ------.

We reached the hotel in good time.

The cabbie coughed to let us know we'd arrived.

A bit embarrassed, I let go of Ajay, who paid the fare.

At the hotel entrance, we met a few of my work-mates who were coming to the party, and I introduced them to Ajay. We walked into the hotel together, and then I went to the ladies room to do up my lipstick, which by now I was sure was messed up; a lot of it was safely deposited all over Ajay's cheeks and face.

I came out of the ladies, wiped his cheek gently free of the lipstick with a tissue that I was carrying, and since it was already well past party-time to begin, we moved towards the banquet room where the party was already in full swing. We have quite a lot of staff in our airline, including the ground-staff and the air-crew. And once you added their guests, we were expecting around seven hundred people at the party.

In the room, there was some great music playing, and people were already shaking a leg on the dance floor.

Although I'd been with the airline for only a few months, I was already quite popular with the girls as well as with the guys, and people were greeting me from all sides. I introduced Ajay to as many people as I could, and I could see most of the girls staring at Ajay with a longing look in their eyes.

That made me feel real good.

Ajay hardly seemed to notice the girls.

It was the guys that seemed to bother him.

Every time a male friend of mine from the airline came up and greeted me with a hug and a peck on the cheek and complimented me on how great I was looking, I could almost feel the steam coming out of Ajay's body. He politely wished the guys when I introduced them to him, but I could see that he was just smiling with his mouth, and not with his eyes.

I hurriedly took his hand and guided him on to the dance floor.

It was the first time ever I was dancing with him, and I wanted to cherish the memory of it for all time, Dear Diary.

How I wished those moments could have lasted forever.

For ever and ever and ever and ever more.

But, Dear Diary, Time is the most fragile and perishable commodity I have ever encountered.

Isn't it an irony, that Time, which seems to stand still so often when you DON'T want it to, suddenly ceases to remain still when you most wished it would do so.

Dancing with Ajay for the first time (little did I know then that it would also be the last), I felt I was dancing on clouds of soft silk.

After a couple of dances, during which the dance floor got almost swollen to capacity, Ajay decided he wanted to take a break. We walked off the floor. I held on tight to his hand. I felt soooooo proud that I was with the most handsome man in the room. (He **really** was.)

All the girls were glancing enviously at me as we looked for a couple of cozy chairs to rest on. In a corner of the room which wasn't too crowded, we found an empty sofa and flopped down.

We sat for a few minutes, chatting about this and that. I was really enjoying myself, being with Ajay after such a long time.

Then suddenly, our quiet corner was full of guys from my airline, who seemed to appear like magic. They'd seen me and come over to say 'Hi'.

A few of them, ignoring Ajay, started asking me to join them on the dance floor.

Ajay didn't look too pleased at this invasion, but I did my best to involve him in the chatter and introduced him to the guys.

"That's Ashutosh, and that's Vinay, and Oh, that's Ricky. And guys, this is Ajay, my **SPECIAL** friend."

I stressed on the word 'special', as I could see signs that Ajay's famous temper was on the boil.

But the guys from my airline didn't seem to be interested in him. They only had eyes for me that evening.

At any other time, such a situation would have thrilled me. After all, Dear Diary, which girl wouldn't be carried away by all this male attention? But at this moment, I just wanted to spend some quality time alone with Ajay. I thought to myself – 'Why couldn't everyone just let us alone?'

But I immediately realised that I was being unreasonable. I couldn't ignore my airline friends and be a spoil-sport at my first airline party.

Then Ricky, one of the guys who was bolder than the rest, took me by the hand and guided me on to the dance floor. I didn't even dare to look at Ajay as I walked on dragging behind Ricky. I knew Ajay would be staring daggers at Ricky and me.

It was a slow number, Ricky held me close, and the song just seemed to drag on and on. My mind was now in a whirl, and my one thought was to get back to Ajay as soon as possible.

But the guys were like a swarm of bees and I was their honey.

They just weren't in the mood to leave me alone.

As soon as the first dance was over, another guy replaced Ricky. He didn't even give me an opportunity to politely refuse.

But as soon as this second dance was over, I rushed off like a sprinter towards Ajay (as fast as my high heels permitted me), before any other guy could grab me or request the pleasure of my company for a dance.

I reached the corner where Ajay was seated. He was trying to look indifferent, but I noticed that his fists were clenched, a sure sign that he was steamed up. As soon as I reached close to him, I tried to hold his hand; but he shook off my gesture.

"I hope you're enjoying yourself", he said. "Inviting me here to escort you and then shoving me aside. What's the big idea? Are you trying to prove to me how popular you are?"

He said this in a loud, harsh voice, which could clearly be heard over the sound of the music by some people seated nearby.

Heads were turning.

Folks were starting to stare at us.

I was blushing with embarrassment as the people who were staring at us included a group of crew members who were my close friends.

I excused myself to Ajay, telling him I had to visit the ladies room.

I started to walk out of the party hall into the lobby of the hotel. I could sense that he was following me as soon as we reached the hotel lobby, and before I could reach the safety of the ladies room, he grabbed my arm and started his one-sided ranting all over again.

We immediately became the centre of attention for all the reception staff and other guests in the lobby. This was something I could really do without, so I shook off his hand and quickly walked out of the hotel lobby and reached the road outside the hotel.

Ajay followed me out there as well and began to air his grievances in public.

Around that time, (it was by now around eight-thirty), the road was quite empty and desolate and Ajay's loud voice could clearly be heard till the end of the quiet road.

I was sure that he'd gulped down a couple of quick drinks while I'd been dancing with the other guys, and he was quite high on alcohol.

I was getting sick of his jealous monologue and just then, I got a call and I thankfully picked it up. Anything which could divert his attention was welcome.

"Where **ARE** you???" said the voice at the other end. It was Maya, my colleague, who I'd seen at the party. "They've just announced the prize for the **MOST STUNNING FEMALE CABIN CREW** and you've won it. Everyone's looking out for you. Where **ARE** you??" she repeated.

Again, at any other time, it would have been a **WOW** moment for me; Preity Singh, small town girl from Dehradun.

But now? My mind couldn't absorb it. I hastily told Maya that I'd just stepped out for some fresh air and would be back in a minute.

Then I looked back at Ajay, and with the intention of changing the topic, I foolishly told him about the prize I'd just been told I'd won.

That made him madder than ever.

He started to scream and abuse me.

"I suppose now you'll have more guys than ever falling over you. That's what you want, isn't it, you bitch?"

And then......, and then......, Dear Diary, words seemed to fail him, so he slapped me, hard, across my cheek.

I was stunned.

I was almost paralysed with shock.

Not satisfied with slapping me once, he raised his hand to strike me again, and I could see it coming towards me, as if in slow motion.

I was staring at him like a chicken stares when hypnotised by a fox, anticipating the hurt, but unable to move, when suddenly, someone grabbed Ajay's hand and stopped it in mid-air.

I turned to look and see who my saviour was.

It was Parth, a purser with my airline, who was on his way to the hotel for the party.

He'd been walking past us to enter the hotel, had taken in the situation at a glance, and realised we were having a lover's tiff.

Lovers?

Hah!!!

By now it was more like a **HATER's** tiff, Dear Diary.

Still holding Ajay's hand in a firm grip (Parth is quite a tough guy himself), Parth asked me in a gentle voice, "Preity, is this guy bothering you?"

I'd momentarily lost my voice in all this excitement, so I merely shook my head to indicate a 'No.'

Then Parth slowly let go Ajay's hand, but stood by, just in case.

For the longest of moments, Parth and Ajay stared at each other, without either of them making a move.

Ajay was staring with burning hatred; Parth staring with cool indifference.

By now I was terrified where all this would lead up to.

It seemed that it just needed a small spark for the situation to explode.

I did the only thing I could do, Dear Diary.

I prayed.

I prayed hard.

Reeeeeal hard.

God heard my prayer.

Thank you, God. Thank you.

I don't know **WHAT** went on in Ajay's mind in those long seconds, but after that staring contest (which he lost), he shifted his gaze away from Parth, looked at me for a split second, turned and walked off without a word.

I could have collapsed with relief, Dear Diary.

I watched him reach the end of the road and then disappear into the distance.

Into the distance, and into memory.

One part of me wanted to call out to him and stop him from walking away.

But fortunately, the sensible and logical part of my brain took over, and I let him go.

I let him walk out of my life. Forever.

There was a limit to which I could tolerate things.

At that moment, I knew it was all over between the two of us.

A thought suddenly raced through my mind.

Was I, Preity Singh, not meant to love, or to be loved?

Ever?

First, the chilled, cold break-off with Manoj. And now, this stormy break up with Ajay.

Was I that bad at keeping a relationship going?

Was it all **my** fault that guys couldn't stick with me?

Surely....surely.....I wasn't that bad a person.

Or was I?

Thinking all these thoughts overloaded the circuits of my brain. These depressing thoughts, combined with the tension of the past few minutes and the pain of the stinging slap I'd received, had been too much for me to handle.

My head spun and I started to fall.

Fortunately, Parth was alert and caught me as I was falling.

"You all right, Preity?" he asked anxiously, with a concerned look on his handsome face. "Should I drop you home?"

I got a hold on myself.

I couldn't just fall to pieces.

After all, I'm a *pahadi* girl.

And we *pahadis* are born tough.

I attempted a weak smile and told him I'd be fine.

We stood there for a couple of minutes till I got my breath back.

Then we walked into the party together.

As soon as I entered, I was surrounded by colleagues congratulating and hugging me.

"Congrats, Most Stunning Female Crew!!!!"

I gracefully acknowledged their wishes and smiled a hollow smile, because I knew I'd won a hollow victory.

I'd lost that six foot tall trophy which I'd so desperately wanted.

The trophy that had just walked out of my life.

That trophy which I had desired above anything else was now out of my reach forever.

Then people nearby started to stare at my face.

Although Ajay had given me just one slap, it had been a hard one. Four red stripes clearly showed through the make-up on my left cheek in the bright lights of the party room.

Also, people had seen me leave the room with Ajay, and now they'd seen me walk in with Parth, with Ajay nowhere around.

Folks must have guessed what had happened and put two and two together, but were thankfully too polite and tactful to ask uncomfortable questions.

I chatted lightly with some friends (though my mind and heart were elsewhere), and moved around the crowd.

Someone pressed a drink into my hand, and I gratefully sipped it. I immediately started to feel a little better when the strong liquid went down my throat.

I could sense Parth hanging around me attentively, not too close and not too far.

Parth. My savior. My knight in shining armour.

I had a little dinner as soon as the buffet counter opened for service. I had mostly salads. I really didn't feel like eating a thing, but I was sensible, and I knew that sleeping on an empty stomach would only add to my problems.

By the time I'd finished my light meal, the party was rocking.

I felt I'd better leave the party as soon as possible. I didn't have Ajay with me any longer to drop me home, and I didn't like the idea of travelling alone too late in public transport with this skimpy dress I had on with all the skin that it showed.

I said a few polite 'byes' to friends and was nearing the exit, when Parth approached me and asked me if I was leaving. When I said yes, he offered to escort me home.

I accepted his offer gratefully, and we walked to where his

car was parked. It was just a few feet away from where we'd both been part of that stormy scene about an hour ago, and I wanted to get away from the bad memories that place held for me as soon as I could.

We got into his car quickly.

Parth asked me where I lived, and we moved off.

For some time, neither of us spoke. Then I broke the ice.

"I'm sorry you had to leave the party early because of me", I said in an apologetic tone.

"Oh, that's perfectly all right", he replied immediately, as if he'd been waiting for me to say that.

He glanced at me and continued – "**I'm** the one who should be thankful. I'm getting to spend time with the most stunning crew member all by myself," he smiled.

It was light, harmless flirting, and although I wasn't really in the mood, we both enjoyed it. It helped me partially take my mind off Ajay as well.

Throughout the drive, Parth behaved like a thorough gentleman and kept me amused with his sense of humour. He was a wonderful conversationalist and was so well informed about a range of interesting topics. Spending time with him was just the medicine I needed.

All too soon we reached my building and he asked me if he could have the pleasure of reaching me to the door of my apartment.

I could make out, Dear Diary, that Parth had started to care for me.

I'll be honest. The feeling from my side was mutual.

But now I was careful about where I was going to deposit my heart.

I wanted to deposit it in a place where there was '**no risk and high returns.**'

Staying in Mumbai for a year has made me think of even love in terms of a monetary transaction. Hee hee.
So I said to myself, 'Slow, Preity, Slow. Take it easy.'
Though I let him escort me all the way up to my doorstep.

We said goodnight there. I was slightly disappointed that he didn't try to kiss me. But in a way I was glad that he didn't. I was in no frame of mind to add on new complications before I'd sorted the old ones out.

I entered my apartment. Anita was stretched out on the living-room sofa, in track pants and a Tee-shirt, watching a music channel on TV and hogging a bowl of noodles.

She glanced up at me in surprise. "Back so early?" she queried.

Then she saw the red mark on my cheek (it was still there, Ajay's last and final imprint on me), and she also saw a couple of tears resting in my eyes.

Anita certainly wasn't tactful about the mark on my cheek or my tears like my colleagues at the party had been.

She wasn't **supposed** to be tactful.

She was my flat-mate.

She was **family**.

She immediately asked me what was wrong.

I told her.

I poured my heart out.

It felt good to have someone to talk to.

Someone to share my heartaches and fears with.

She listened to every word I spoke.

She's a great listener.

After I had finished, she put her arms around me and didn't say a word.

Her silence and warm embrace gave me more comfort than a whole dictionary full of words could have ever done.

"There's always hope, Preity", she said. "Don't give up. God has made someone, somewhere, who's just right for a sweet girl like you. And till you find him, you'll have to keep on looking. And if you look hard enough and don't give up, ever, he'll be waiting for you, Preity, with open arms and an open heart. Believe me. That's a universal truth."

And with those words of hope ringing in my ears, Dear Diary, I went to bed with a lighter heart and dreamed of Parth.

Date : 10th November

As usual, Dear Diary, every trouble brings its learnings with it. We only need to be wise enough to learn from it.

I learnt a lot on this day, Dear Diary. A reeeeeal, reeeeeeal lot.

So although there was a lot of pain involved, Dear Diary, the evening of the party taught me some priceless lessons.

I learnt that the faster you rush into a relationship, the faster you're likely to rush out.

I realised that there is a limit to the nonsense that a person should take from anyone else.

I also realised that it isn't worth sacrificing all other relationships for the sake of one unreasonable person, however much your heart tells you that you love that person.

I learnt, Dear Diary, that relationships are like little children. They have to be nurtured.

I also learnt that relationships are like glass. They are brittle and fragile. Easily broken.

And I learnt that great relationships have a spark of the divine. They take you to a higher realm.

And although I'm in no hurry, Dear Diary, I feel it in my bones that the next relationship I will be part of is going to be a greeeeeat one.

Date : 5th January

Appraisal by a Monster

Dear Diary,

I'm sorry if my handwriting today lacks my normal strength and confidence, but I just feel sooooo low.

Sooooo down.

I can't believe that such a thing that I'm about to tell you can happen. It's the first time that I'm starting to have second thoughts about this career I've chosen.

I'm sorry, Dear Diary, I don't mean to sound negative. But let me explain what's happened in the last couple of days and then maybe you'll understand and excuse me.

You know my colleague, Bina, right? I've told you about her. She's recently joined our airline and is still on her training flights. She hasn't got her 'wings' as yet.

She's from Chandigarh. Very good looking girl.

Slim, tall, doe-eyed, veeeeeery fair, long black silky hair which I've always envied, sharp straight nose, classical Indian features. She really should have been a model. But she's quite shy and introverted by nature. She's a very nice person, and maybe that's why people tend to push her around a lot.

Well, on the last flight me and Bina did together, we flew to Hyderabad. It was a check-flight for Bina, as she's still not completed her training. The flight had been delayed at take-off and landed in Hyderabad around midnight, and for some reason or the other I was so tired, that as soon as I reached my hotel room, I went off to the land of dreams.

I didn't order a snack or even a juice from room service. I didn't spend time gossiping with the girls as we normally do. But I woke up really refreshed for the early morning flight back to Mumbai.

Poor Bina. She wasn't so fortunate. If I'd known what she was going through that night, I would have given up my sleep and would have rushed to her help.

I wouldn't allow anyone to push me around the way she was pushed around. But maybe that's why she was picked on. People know that she's just too timid and meek. An easy target. The fact that she's a real beauty doesn't hurt them either.

But I'm rushing ahead with the story, Dear Diary. I know you like to get the facts in order and not jumbled up. But I'm soooo pissed off with what's happened, I just can't help it. Anyway, I'll try to go in sequence.

Bina was looking harassed and pale throughout the morning return flight to Mumbai. But I was so busy serving passengers that I really had no time to ask the poor girl if anything was wrong.

Well, after we landed, I went off to my apartment. I wanted to catch up on my reading. I'd just picked up the latest Archie comic where Archie proposes to Betty, and I couldn't wait to see how it went. I've grown up on Archie and the gang and feel I know them as well as I know my own family.

Archie and Betty. Getting married. A love story made in heaven. So thrilling.

Anyway, that's not what is important now.

I'd just reached the part where Archie was about to propose, and my mobile rang. I had half a mind not to even see who was calling. Whoever it was could wait. Archie and Betty come first. But then, mom hasn't been keeping too well lately, and I was worried that it could be someone from home on the line.

Archie may come a close second, but family is first.

It wasn't from home. It was Bina's number flashing. "Now what the freak does she want", was my initial irritated reaction. But I decided to pick it up. She normally doesn't call for small talk, and also I remembered her pale face in the morning on the flight and was worried that something may be wrong.

Something **WAS** wrong.

Drastically wrong.

I picked up the phone and before I could complete saying, "Hi Beens", (I call her Beens, Dear Diary, it suits her so well), she burst into tears. Like, I mean, she was really sobbing her heart out.

I got scared. What was up, I wondered?

"Hey Beens, take it easy", I said. "Nothing can be that bad. Tell me what's the matter."

Through her sobs, she conveyed that she didn't want to speak about it over the phone.

She asked if I could meet her somewhere in private, where she could speak to me in person. She asked me if I could come over to her apartment which she shared with another couple of girls. She said the girls were both on flights and she was alone at home, (her room-mates were both cabin-crew as well), and she sounded desperate that I reach there fast.

I wondered why she wanted **me** to help her with whatever was the matter.

Although she is a very nice and sweet natured person, I wasn't really a close friend of hers. But then I guess Beens has no special close friend in this city.

She's been here for two months, and although that's not a long time, there are many girls who make a huge gang of friends within that period.

But Beens is so shy and reserved, that as soon as her training day is over or her flight lands, she just rushes back to her apartment. In the two months that she's been training with our airline, she hasn't attended a single informal get-together that we cabin-crew have organised. She seldom speaks to us about her family or friends back home, unlike the rest of us girls who do so whenever we get a chance.

So I didn't hesitate when she called me over, but just slipped into my jeans and a Tee-shirt, ran a comb through my thick, untidy hair, rushed out and caught a rickshaw, and was at her place within fifteen minutes. She opened the door, still sobbing, and flung herself into my arms.

What she told me made me forget about Archie and Betty.

No, what it did was make me **hate** Archie. It made me hate the whole race of men. (Well, maybe not **ALL** men. I couldn't **ever** imagine someone like Parth, for example, doing anything like this to anyone, even if he had the power to do so.) But how **COULD** any man do something like this. And that too to a sweetheart like Beens?

But I'm rushing ahead of the story again.

I first told her to relax, and went into her kitchen and made two mugs of hot, steaming lemon tea.

Mom always says that step one to solving any problem is to first prepare and then slowly sip a cup of hot lemon tea.

The very act of making the tea calms you down, and once you feel the nice hot lemon tea, (I prefer mine with honey), going down your insides, it's such a comforting feeling, that it helps you look at any problem in a refreshed and relaxed light.

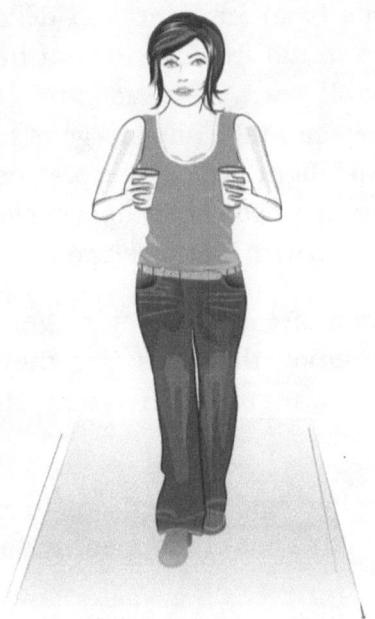

I gave Beens a mug which she gratefully took and sipped. I started to sip mine, and then listened to what she had to say.

When Beens had finished half her mug of tea and had finally calmed down enough to speak without bursting into tears, I understood what had upset her so much.

Let me explain to you what happened, Dear Diary.

Let me start at the beginning.

As I said, Beens joined the world of flying just a couple of months ago.

I started flying just six months ago myself, but I've always been a tomboy and I've adjusted well into this hectic life.

But poor Beens is so feminine and delicate. Not only in looks, but also in nature. One look at her and men start getting ideas. All sorts of ideas. And they instinctively realise that they can take advantage of her. She's not the kind who would fight back. She just can't. It's not her nature. Fortunately, so far, people have been kind. The crew she has flown with have been good guys.

Most cabin crew **are** good people. Very nice and kind hearted. They enjoy their fun but they're not cruel. If someone doesn't want to join in a game, they let the person be.

But you have a bad egg, a rotten egg, in every bunch. And the rotten egg in this basket happens to be a senior purser.

A guy named Nimesh.

No. A swine named Nimesh.

He's not a human being by any standards.

Anyway, what happened was this.

Let me explain how our industry functions, Dear Diary. Then you'll get a better idea as to what I'm telling you.

In the aviation industry, we have a hierarchy in the cabin-crew.

At the top, we have the senior steward/purser. He is in charge of all the cabin-crew aboard every flight.

Then we have the bulk of the cabin-crew serving the passengers, who are experienced guys.

And then we have freshers or trainees like Beens. The freshers are appraised or evaluated on their performance on the job for the first few flights by the senior steward who is there with them on flight.

Some areas on which the evaluation of trainee-crew is done are things like being polite with the passengers, being attentive to their needs, being efficient in food and beverage service and so on.

And then, if the appraisal report shows that the trainee steward or hostess has been doing a good job, is efficient while serving food and drink, polite to the passengers and all that, the trainee is confirmed as a permanent crew member.

Obviously, every fresher is anxious to get good reports or appraisals; because a single black mark, a single negative report by any Senior Steward (who's the person who conducts these appraisals), which says that the fresher was rude to a passenger, or lazy or slow or inefficient in performing the in-flight duties, could mean trouble for the fresher.

A couple of negative reports would ensure that the fresher is terminated before he or she is made permanent. Every fresher is aware of this.

It's the end of a dream for them if that happens.

I was fortunate, Dear Diary, that when I was a fresher, I flew with senior stewards who were nice guys. Fair and honest. Decent chaps. They went out of their way to help freshers learn the job and covered up for any mistakes we made.

I made a couple of mistakes myself as a fresher, but that's another story.

The point is, I had some real good guardian angels as my seniors, and today I'm a confirmed cabin-crew with a secure job. I've paid off the loan that papa had taken to put me through the airline course. Now I'm sending some amount of money home every month. I'm also putting aside a fixed amount every month in a bank fixed-deposit for my future. And I spend on my clothes and food and entertainment as well. It gets you fairly good money, along with the allowances, being a cabin-crew.

Every fresher hopes to do all this with their salary as soon as they're confirmed, and a bad appraisal means that all these hopes of a secure life for themselves and their family go right out of the window.

That's a biiiiig price to pay. Everyone in the industry knows that.

And there are a few swines who are just waiting for opportunities to take advantage of this fact. One of these swines is the senior steward, Nimesh.

I was aware that although Beens comes from a very aristocratic family (they're descended from royalty), her particular branch of the family has recently fallen on bad times, and are financially close to ruin. Beens is their one hope of getting some type of financial security and paying the tuition fees of her younger brother and sister.

Beens lost her father early on in life, and has no support from any of her uncles or aunts. In fact, it is these relatives who've conned her mother out of their rightful share of family wealth.

Her mother has scraped together every rupee that she could to make sure that Beens could enroll in a cabin-crew course and get a stable job with an airline. Because of this troubled and disturbed background, Beens has developed an introverted personality.

Beens cleared the cabin-crew course, and with her natural beauty, etiquette and grace, she easily got selected as a trainee cabin-crew with our airline. She's worked hard at the job and at her training, even reporting for work when she's been unwell. She's really dedicated, and I admire her for these qualities. She never has a negative word to say about anybody or anything.

Well, on this particular training flight of hers, Beens made a small mistake while serving beverages.

There was some slight turbulence, and twice during the flight Beens spilt a little coffee that she was in the process of serving onto a couple of passengers. The male passenger was cool about the issue. He didn't even say a word. In fact he smiled and told Beens not to worry.

But the female on whom Beens spilt maybe a couple of drops of coffee made a scene. She was a real bitch. She yelled and screamed at poor Beens for not being careful, and Nimesh, who was nearby, saw and heard the whole thing.

It wasn't anything major. It was something which any other Senior Steward would have soothed over and covered up.

But not Nimesh. I think he was just waiting for such an opportunity, and it fell right into his lap.

Before the flight landed, he managed to get Beens alone in the service area of the plane and yelled the shit out of her. She was already pale when the flight landed late at night in Hyderabad, but since none of us had heard the yelling that Nimesh had given her, we didn't think much of her pale and haggard appearance. We were all too eager to rush off to our hotel rooms and go off to the land of dreams.

After the flight landed at Hyderabad, we reached the hotel where we crew were supposed to put up for the night. It's quite a nice hotel. Comfy and homely. As I mentioned earlier, I was dog-tired, and I rushed up to my room. (As the hotel was relatively empty, and we crew have good relations with the hotel staff, we all requested for and were allocated individual rooms.) I changed into my nightie and crashed. I immediately went out like a light, and only awoke the next morning when the alarm went off at six.

But what Beens went through on that night was terrible.

This is what she said happened.

She said that she checked into her hotel room around half past midnight, the same time that all the rest of us went to our rooms.

She was still upset about the error in service she had committed during the flight and the yelling she'd received from Nimesh, and was pondering over it in her room, when suddenly someone knocked at her hotel room door.

By then, it was almost one a.m.

Beens went to the door, looked through the peep-hole, recognised Nimesh who was standing outside the door, and she unthinkingly opened the door to let him in.

He stepped into her room, latched the door shut from the inside, and sat himself down on the bed.

Beens stood near the door, trembling, and shakingly asked him what he wanted.

"You", burst out Nimesh, cackling like a hyena.

Beens could smell alcohol on his breath even from the distance where she was standing. He'd obviously had a few pegs once he'd checked into his room.

"What,-----what did you say?" Beens asked hesitatingly.

She couldn't believe her ears. What exactly did he mean, she thought to herself?

This man was supposed to be her senior, her mentor, her guide. He couldn't be talking this crazy stuff. Maybe she'd heard him wrong.

Suddenly Nimesh swiftly got up, grabbed Beens' hand, twisted it hard, and dragged her down, forcing her to sit on the bed close beside him.

"Now, listen to what I say. And listen carefully", rasped Nimesh to Beens, his hand still tightly gripping her delicate arm.

"I'm not going to force you to do anything you won't agree to. I'm not stupid. I don't want any problems. Just as **YOU** don't want any problems either, do you? I'm sure we can come to some sort of agreement. A mutual understanding, eh Bina?" Nimesh leered at her, his boozed breath hitting her dainty, aristocratic nose and almost making her sick.

"I----I really don't understand what you mean", stammered Beens, almost close to fainting by now.

"Why, it's quite simple", said the brute. "You're a smart girl. Do I need to spell it out for you? I've had my eye on you since the day you joined the airline. A friend of mine and me spotted you together on your first day of training. We were wondering which of us would be the fortunate one to supervise you on your training flight. I've even had your financial background checked out. You need this job desperately, right?"

Beens merely nodded nervously. She was beyond speech by now.

"Well", continued Nimesh, who obviously wasn't short of words himself, "You won't be keeping this job for long if you don't co-operate."

Beens looked at him, puzzled.

He continued – "I've got something that you want. Something that you want desperately. Your appraisal. Which is totally in my hands. You want a good appraisal, don't you? I'll be filling up your appraisal for the training flight tomorrow. And you haven't made it any easier for yourself by making that stupid mistake you made on flight. I can really blow it up out of all proportion in my appraisal report. Guest complaints against trainees are viewed real seriously. I've noted the name and address of the female passenger you spilt coffee on. This could be the last flight you ever make. But I'm not a bad guy at heart, you know. I'm pretty understanding by nature. I'm really a nice guy. I don't want to see you screw up your career. We could do a deal. I give you a good appraisal. I overlook your mistake. But everything has a price tag, you know? You can't expect free lunches in life. Look at it this way, I'm teaching you a valuable lesson about life. Oh, don't worry. I don't need any money. What I want isn't gonna cost you a paisa. In fact you just might enjoy it".

He put his other arm around her shoulder and turned her face to his.

Poor Beens went into a state of shock. Her mind went numb. There are many girls today who think nothing about going all the way before marriage, either for fun or to secure their career, but Beens wasn't one of them. She belonged to the old school of thought. And she retained old school family values.

She wanted desperately to resist, but panic had temporarily taken away even her voice.

And that beast, drunk with liquor and lust, obviously went by the maxim that silence implies consent.

Before she knew what was happening, she was on the bed and he was on top of her.

That's when Beens fainted.

When she woke up from her faint, she was alone in her room. Her clothes were scattered over the floor. She felt a dull pain inside her.

The clock on the hotel room wall showed four-thirty in the morning.

Beens began to sob. She didn't know what to do. She didn't know who to call for help. She didn't have a close friend in the crew who she could wake up and confide in.

Nimesh had been right about one thing. She needed to keep this job at any cost.

And anyway, if she brought up the issue, it would just be her word against his.

A trainee's word against that of a senior supervisor. She lacked self-confidence and doubted that her word would carry much weight with the authorities, who anyway would wish to avoid a scene to save the airline from a scandal.

Ultimately, her nervous nature wouldn't let her make a scene and bring the whole thing to light. This was just what that swine had counted on.

She couldn't go back to sleep. So she took a hot shower to wash herself of her guilt, put on her uniform in a daze, and shuffled down to the hotel coffee shop for a hot cup of coffee to bring some life to her dulled senses.

By then, it was five-thirty in the morning, and she was the only guest in the hotel coffee shop. She was served a strong cup of coffee, which she slowly and mechanically sipped, staring straight ahead like a zombie.

Fortunately, her tears had dried up by now, and she had the presence of mind to gulp down a couple of calming pills which she always carried in her purse.

When the rest of us crew started moving into the coffee shop around six-thirty for our breakfast, we noticed Beens sitting quietly at a corner table. Since she didn't look too cheerful, everyone avoided her, including, Dear Diary, I am ashamed to tell you, myself.

Nimesh entered the coffee shop and shoveled a huge breakfast onto his plate from the buffet counter. I ignored him as I'd always found him creepy. If I'd only known then what I know now, I would have raised the roof in that coffee shop.

But we were all too absorbed in our gossip and chatter to notice that poor Beens needed help, and needed it badly.

I sat at a table with my friends in that crew, Tony and Sushmita. Tony's from Goa, a handsome dude who looks more like a tanned Hollywood hero, and he's got a tremendous sense of humour.

He had me and Sush rolling in laughter over breakfast with his one-liners. He's too witty, and when he starts picking on someone and mimicking them, we feel he's wasting his talent. He ought to be on stage, entertaining crowds of thousands. But then, we wouldn't be able to afford a front row seat at his performances, so maybe it is better for us this way.

Sush is from Kolkota, a typical sweet looking Bong with a sweet tooth, but somehow she never seems to put on an ounce, let alone kilograms. I could just kill her for that, if she weren't a friend of mine. She's about a couple of years old in the airline, which makes her senior to me, but she's very down to earth and good fun to be with.

She's having an affair with a pilot who's married, but that's her personal life. Somehow she manages to get herself rostered for flights with her pilot boyfriend pretty often. On such occasions, she rarely has a minute to spare for the rest of us, but on trips like this one, where her special pilot friend wasn't part of our crew, me and Sush ended up sharing our meal tables together.

We each had a lovely breakfast of succulent cheese omelettes, croissants and I had my cup of early morning hot chocolate (extra sweet), as usual.

Well, in short, we totally ignored poor Beens, and walked out of the coffee shop laughing, with not a care in the world.

We boarded the crew bus. The hotel staff as usual handled our luggage.

On the short drive to the airport, I finally took notice of Beens, sitting huddled up in a single seat at the front of the crew coach, arms folded across her front. I went up to her and asked her if she was feeling all right. She nodded briefly, and didn't seem interested in conversation. I shrugged and went back to join Sush.

We reached the airport, got down, collected our bags, passed through the security check, boarded the flight, and the rest – Well, I've already mentioned that before.

It was a pretty uneventful morning flight back to Mumbai, with Beens this time doing her work without any mistake, but without a smile on her beautiful face. I wondered even then how closely she resembled some tragedy queen of yesteryear.

Now, back to the present, Dear Diary.

Beens finished telling me this sorry tale, sobbing. She said – "I just want to quit the job, Preity, only I can't afford to. My family is depending on me. I just didn't know what to do. My mind has been numb ever since -----. But after I returned to my apartment today morning, I suddenly thought of turning to you for help, Preity. I'm sorry to involve you in my personal problems, but there was really no one else I could think of. I've always admired you ever since I met you, Preity, you're so --- so ----- **CONFIDENT**."

Now that Beens had poured her heart out to me, I sat aghast. My first thoughts were how to make sure that

Nimesh, the senior steward, was thrown out of the airline as soon as possible.

I'd go up to him and slap his face.

I'd demand a meeting with our Managing Director.

I'd go to the press.

I'd,----I'd-----, Oh, there were **so** many things I wanted to do all at once, I didn't know where to start.

I was burning with rage.

Poor Beens was frightened to see the look on my face. But that's the way I'm made.

You know, Dear Diary, I mentioned to you once long ago when I was in junior college in Dehradun, and a college guy had tried to push me around, how I'd blasted him in the canteen. Poor guy rarely turned up in college after that day.

I calmed down, and realised I needed to be practical.

Beens told me that she couldn't afford to lose her job. That was her priority.

If she made a formal complaint, or if I created a scene on her behalf, there would be an official enquiry. Nimesh, who was well connected with the airline management, would pull his strings to ensure that Beens backed down or faced further harassment at work. She could possibly be suspended without pay till the enquiry was complete.

It would be just her word against his, and although we both knew she was in the right, unfortunately that's not the way the world works.

I was at a loss for what to do, so I called Sush and asked her if she could come over to Beens' apartment. Although she was apparently asleep when I called, judging by her yawns over the phone, (Sush loves her nap, she's so like a cat in many ways), when she sensed the urgency in my voice, she said she'd be over within an hour.

In the meantime, I got Beens to relax, put on some lively music on her system, made another hot cup of tea for both of us, and chatted to her brightly about the recent Salman Khan film I'd seen.

Beens lightened up. She could see I was making an effort to cheer her up, and she was grateful.

I looked around the apartment that Beens shared with two other Punjabi air-hostesses, one of whom was her cousin. Both the girls were abroad on flights and wouldn't be back for another couple of days at least.

The apartment was pleasant. The living room was done up in a tasteful lemon yellow. There were bean bags scattered around the room, and a colourful Kashmiri rug on the floor, which gave the room a very warm and cheerful look.

The kitchen too was spick and span. I'm sure that was Beens at work, keeping it clean. Whoever she marries is going to be a real fortunate guy in every way. I just hope he appreciates what he's getting and takes care of Beens. Poor girl, she could use a nice slice of good fortune in her life. She's been through quite a bad patch recently. But as they say, the darkest hour is before the dawn.

Anyway, it was a very pleasant looking and well kept apartment; a bit more well kept than mine. Although mom's been after me since a young age to pick up good housekeeping skills, somehow when there's no one around to nag me, I barely manage to tidy up my bed and wash the dinner dishes.

The other girls I share the apartment with aren't too bad, but they've all got hectic jobs and are hard pressed for time. Sometimes I end up making their beds and washing their dishes as well. But I can't complain. They're good to me and have done so much for me in their own way. Like the time I was down with flu and feeling miserable. Anita, the one who's in advertising, actually took a couple of days off from work to nurse me back to health. I was really touched. She took me to the doctor, bought my medicines and made sure I took them on time, made piping hot soup every couple of hours, and kept me company for the entire two days, even canceling a movie date with her boyfriend.

Then I had a brainwave. My flat-mate Payal, who shares Anita's room (me and Khushboo share the other room), was leaving us for the next six months as the airline she flew with was promoting her and posting her to Dubai for a stint.

We'd have one empty bed in our apartment.

I'd ask Beens to move in. She'd be well looked after, and our apartment would get a touch of class. Win-Win. I was sure the other two girls in my apartment wouldn't mind once they met Beens. She's a darling.

Eyes gleaming, I asked Beens if she'd like to move in with us.

She stared, then broke into a beaming smile. Rarely have I seen a smile of such pure, genuine and innocent heartfelt joy on anyone's face.

It made my day.

No. It made my year.

"Well", I asked Beens. "What's your answer?" knowing fully well what her answer was.

"When could I move in?" was her immediate response.

She went on to add that although one of the girls she currently stayed with was her cousin, and both the girls were very nice, they had little time for Beens or even for each other. In the first place, both of them were flying with international airlines, and spent a lot of time overseas. And secondly, they both had their boyfriends in Mumbai with whom they spent most of their time when they were not flying.

So poor Beens, a girl who badly needed support and company, was almost always on her own.

"You could move in within a couple of days", I smiled, happy that it was working out so well. "That's when Payal is leaving, and you could take her place. She's going to be in Dubai for at least six months, so for the next half year at least, you'll be part of our family. You, me, Anita and Khushboo. You'll love being with us. Anita works for an advertising agency and Khushboo is a model and acts in serials. They're both great girls and really supportive. And of course, I'll be there as well. Come on, let's call your mom and tell her the news. Don't mention to her the problem you had with Nimesh. She'll be worried sick and would ask you to leave your job. Just don't worry about it. I'll make sure he damn well won't try anything like that with you again, or for that matter with any other girl. I'm not rostered for flying for the next two days and neither are you, so I can help you to pack and shift. It'll be fun."

Beens started getting infected by my excitement, opened her cupboard, and started to get a few of her clothes and things out so she could be ready to pack them. She planned to inform her cousin, who was her room-mate, about her decision to shift, as soon as her cousin returned from her flight. "I'm sure she won't mind", said Beens. "She's so outgoing and popular that getting another room-mate in my place won't be any problem for her."

I helped her sort out her things.

I also wanted to discuss her problem with Sush and Tony, both of whom I was sure would be supportive.

Beens wasn't too eager to share the incident with them as she didn't know them too well and felt a bit overawed by them as they were seniors, but I assured her they were good people, and would help in finding a solution to the problem. The immediate problem being of course, how to tactfully get a strong message across to Nimesh that he better not try anything like this with Beens ever again, and to make sure that he didn't mess up her future appraisals if she didn't continue to 'co-operate' with him, as he had so crudely put it.

We had to be very careful that the whole thing didn't rebound and backfire on poor Beens. At any cost, she shouldn't lose her job or have a black mark against her name at this early stage of her career.

I called Sush, asked her where she'd reached, and told her to call Tony and ask him to come over as well if possible. I told her it was important. She readily agreed and said that she'd co-ordinate with Tony.

I ordered some pizzas for all of us, and some garlic bread with cheesy dip. A full stomach is always a good starting point for problem solving, that's what I feel.

Me and Beens continued sorting out her stuff prior to packing. At least it kept her mind occupied, and that was what I wanted.

By now Beens was gaily chatting to me about her family, her mom, her kid sister and brother, and their house back home. I was glad she was opening up, and I listened attentively, asking appropriate questions now and then.

Talking was good therapy for Beens, and she was soon back to her normal sweet self.

The pizzas arrived, and while I was paying off the delivery guy, Sush and Tony walked in as well. Talk about perfect timing. "Mmmm", said Sush the foodie, inhaling the aroma of freshly baked pizza.

We sat down at the table, and Beens brought us some cans of coke from the fridge. Once each of us had gobbled the first hot cheesy slice, Tony brought up the question as to why he and Sush been called over. "Not that I'm complaining", he said. "It's a pleasure to be having lunch with three such lovely ladies."

"Oh shut up, Tony", said Sush. "Save your dialogue for the girls who don't know you well. Maybe they'll be impressed."

"Now", continued Sush, "what's the matter, Preity? Why are we here? You said it was important."

Beens cast her eyes down at the floor, ashamed at the topic being brought up with Sush and Tony listening.

"Relax, Beens", I soothed her. "What's happened is not your fault in the least. I know Sush and Tony well, and I've called them here for their help and advice."

I then went on with the entire tale. They listened without interrupting. They looked upset at the end of it, but they didn't seem surprised.

"It's a bad thing that's happened, Preity", said Sush, "but it doesn't shock us. You're comparatively new to our airline, and so is Beens. But me and Tony have been around for some time. And these things happen. We've heard Nimesh's name mixed up in this type of misbehaviour before. But there's never been anything concrete. It's always been gossip and grapevine. Very few girls who've been molested will stand up and take the issue further. Most girls know that they'd either lose their jobs, or at least be grounded for some time while the allegation is sorted out. If misbehaviour isn't proved against the guy, the girl loses her job for putting a false allegation. Even if her word **is** taken, it's still a scandal that no girl would like to be a part of. Some girls just quit their job in despair after such an incident, as it spoils the whole concept of a career in aviation for them. So although these things happen once in a while when dogs like Nimesh are around, sadly, they always seem to get away with it. What's worse is, once they have a girl in their clutches, they keep on at her till they get tired of her and till they find someone new who catches their fancy."

"That's **exactly** what we need your advice on", I said. "How do we get this guy to stop picking on Beens in future, without giving her a bad appraisal out of spite for having confided in us? He'll be submitting her appraisal by tomorrow latest, and if he realises she's confided in us, he'll mess up her appraisal. And even if tomorrow's appraisal goes through well, Beens still has some more training to go, and he'll surely schedule himself on the same flight as her again. For Beens' sake, we don't want this made public."

"I think I can help", said Tony. "I don't exactly gel with this guy Nimesh, and I've heard these sort of rumours about him before. He's from my batch. We both joined the airline around six years ago and did our training together. He's risen fast because he's got some uncle who's a director in the airline. And that's why he's so confident of throwing his weight around. But he doesn't mess with me and a couple of my friends from my batch, as he knows we can be pretty tough when we want to. I'd say this is not a job for you girls. I'll go along with these two friends of mine and meet Nimesh. You know these guys, Sashank and Ravi. You've flown with them. They're both nice guys and they'll join me. They don't like that creep either. We'll make sure that he gets the message straight and strong that Beens is off-limits. She's part of our group, and if he messes with her, he messes with all of us. We'll also make sure he puts nothing adverse in her appraisal either today or in the future. I think that will solve the problem without aggravating it."

"I'll come along as well", said Sush. "I'll give this guy a piece of my mind."

"That's precisely why I don't want you along", said Tony. "We're going to put this to Nimesh without any yelling. A low but hard voice is more effective than loud yelling in a situation like this. In fact I better do this right away, before he puts in a negative report about Beens. You never know what his warped mind is capable of doing. Thanks for the pizza, guys. See ya. Take care Beens, and don't worry about a thing. You're under our wing now." He hugged all of us and left.

"Thank God that for every swine like Nimesh, there is a great guy like Tony to counter him", I said.

"Amen", said Sush.

"Thanks a lot guys, you were wonderful", said Beens, with all her heart.

And that was that.

Tony called up that evening and told us that the matter was settled.

He even told us that Nimesh would be calling up Beens to apologise.

What Tony and his friends said to Nimesh to make him agree to apologise, he didn't say, and we didn't ask. Some things are best left unsaid.

But it must have made Nimesh think twice about repeating his gross behavior. Because he actually called Beens and apologised and said he wasn't in his senses that night when he molested her. Of course, he added, she would be getting a good appraisal from his end. Beens heard him out as we'd advised her, said a brief "Okay", and then hung up.

He neither bothered her, nor to the best of our knowledge, any other girl ever again.

I still felt that he'd got off lightly, but considering the circumstances, I guess it was the best that could be done. The matter was resolved without creating any further problem for Beens, and that's what was important. I guess this was preferable to all of us, as compared to visiting courts as witnesses for the next ten years of our lives.

The long and the short of it, Dear Diary, was that I got a lovely person as a new flat-mate, Beens found a new family in Mumbai, and Sush and Tony became close friends to both of us.

Date : 29th January

Dear Diary
Beens has moved into my apartment

Living with us has been like a health tonic for
Beens.

She's simply glowing with confidence.

She's standing up for herself, and has become
positively assertive. No one would ever dare trying
messing with Beens ever again. I'm sure she'd lash
out like a tigeress.

All the same, although she's so self-reliant now, she
still thanks God for the decision she made to call me
up on that fateful day, when her life had descended
to a living hell.

And, Dear Diary, there's so much I've learnt from
this entire appraisal episode concerning Beens.

I've learnt the value of being self-confident, and not
timid. Merely looking confident, standing

straight, looking people straight in the eye, generates a feeling of confidence and tells the other person that this is not someone to be messed with.

I've learnt that just as there are bad people around, waiting to take advantage, so there are diamonds and gems like Tony, ready to help anyone in need.

I've learnt that in-spite of all we say about women's lib, (and it's got many plus points), sometimes it does take a man to do the job.

I've learnt, Dear Diary, that when I'm in a situation where I need help, I shouldn't hesitate, but call my good friends and let them know I'm in trouble.

I've also learnt that at times its preferable to take a subtle approach to solving a problem, rather than barging at it head-on. Of course, it helps if you've got your priorities right.

And most of all Dear Diary, I've realised that whatever be the problem, a good, steaming hot mug of tea always makes the burden easier to bear.

Date : 16th February

Anita's Boyfriend Problem

Dear Diary
What is love?

I mean, why does love exist?

Why was this emotion created?

Isn't love meant to uplift the people who are in love?

Make them feel good about being together?

Aren't two people in love supposed to become one?

In mind?

In thought?

In deed?

For ever and ever and evermore?

That's what the books say. (Don't ask me which books, Dear Diary. All the romantic novels I've ever read say so.)

That's what our parents and elders also say.

And our parents are supposed to be smart people. Who've seen and experienced life.

So then how come in this very important area of life, that of 'love', they are so wrong?

So very wrong?

So very, very wrong?

Or, is it that what our parents speak of is **true** love, and what our generation is experiencing is only **attraction**?

A fatal attraction?

So could our parents be right after all?

I don't know, Dear Diary. I just-------don't------know.

I know only one thing for sure.

And that is, at this moment, I am totally confused.

I better explain why I'm sounding so cynical, Dear Diary. Because I'm normally such a positive person.

I'd better start at the beginning.

Today got off to a good start. I'd returned from a flight yesterday evening. No flights for me today and tomorrow. Two days of pure relaxation. I could get up whenever I liked.

I'd no major plans for the day.

I planned to just generally laze around.

Maybe go for a movie and dinner with Parth later in the day. There's this new Hollywood block-buster movie that's just been released which I've been dying to see.

So I woke up peacefully around nine-thirty.

Opened my eyes and s-t-r-e-t-c-h-e-d.

Relaxed in bed till ten.

Then I lazily got out of bed, went to the kitchen and made myself a nice breakfast of corn flakes with cold milk and honey. Tossed a chopped banana and a few raisins into the bowl. Buttered a couple of slices of toast and added jam and cheese on top. I'd work it all off at the gym later, so I didn't feel guilty about all the calories I was piling in.

I was all alone in the apartment. I didn't exactly know where all three of my roomies were. Hadn't seen any of them since I returned late last evening.

I knew that Beens was on a flight and wouldn't be back for a couple of days.

Khushboo had mentioned that her unit was going for a shoot to some hill station. Maybe she stayed the night there.

And I guessed Anita would have been with her boyfriend. She's crazy about him, and she now spends most of her spare time with him. And sometimes she spends the night with him in his farm-house at Lonavala. So I wasn't surprised that she hadn't turned up at home last night.

Anyway, the fact was that I was alone. And although it's nice to have your friends around, sometimes it's simply heaven to be by yourself.

Alone with yourself and your thoughts.

I carried my breakfast to the table in the living room. Picked up an Archie comics digest, and flipped through it while chewing the toast.

Yum.

I was just having pleasant visions about me and Parth at the movie in the evening, followed by the two of us having a dreamy, romantic candlelight dinner, when the pleasant vision was shattered.

Anita opened the door (rather I'd say she thrust open the door), giving me a rude shock.

She stormed into the apartment, and slammed the door shut.

She didn't even seem to notice me.

"I hate him, I hate him, I hate him, I simply **HATE** him," she cried, flinging herself onto a sofa, and burying her face into a pillow.

I left my half eaten breakfast and rushed to comfort her.

"Hey, hey, hey, Anita. Nothing can be that bad. What's wrong? Tell me."

I tried to pull her face out of the pillow, but she started beating me with her fists.

"Leave me alone", she shrieked. "Just ----- leave ----- me----- alone."

"All right", I said soothingly. "All right. Chill. Relax."

I moved away, giving her space.

I sat down on the opposite sofa, watching her intently.

Whatever had gone wrong, I knew she had to get it out of her system.

There was no use me trying to calm her down while she was still letting off steam.

These situations remind me of a pressure cooker. While the whistle is blowing and the cooker is letting of steam, the only sensible thing to do is to stand back and let it release all the steam within. Only after all the built-in pressure is released, can the cooker be handled and safely opened.

Anita kept sobbing quietly for another five minutes.

Then she suddenly stopped, as if switched off.

She got off the sofa.

With a determined look on her face, she strode swiftly into the kitchen.

I followed her, puzzled and somehow worried by the grim expression on her face.

I thought maybe she wanted a glass of water, and I offered to get it for her and told her to relax. She didn't seem to hear me or even realise that I was around.

She pulled open the drawer of the kitchen cabinet, brought out a knife in her right hand, and attempted to slash her left wrist. I gasped.

For a split second, I stood stunned, watching the scene unfold before me like a slow motion shot in a thriller movie.

Fortunately, that split second was all the time I took to grasp the situation and react.

I was close enough to her to just reach out and grab her right wrist which held the knife, before she could do further damage to herself.

Already I could see a trickle of blood flow from her left wrist where the knife had begun its evil journey of cutting into skin.

Anita twisted my hand away, and kicked me on my left knee with full force.

"Let me be. I don't want to live", she screamed.

Her kick caught me off-guard and I staggered back towards the wall.

She once again attempted to complete the macabre task she had undertaken, and would surely have succeeded in her crazy scheme, if it were not for providence taking a hand.

Providence made a thick curtain of her silky long hair fall over her eyes at the critical moment, and as a reflex action, she raised her right hand (the hand which held the knife), to flick the annoying lock of hair back over her head.

In this moment, I seized my chance, rushed forward, and gave her a stinging slap across her left cheek. I immediately repeated one more slap for good measure.

She dropped the knife, cried out in shock and pain, and fell to her knees, holding the burning cheek with her right hand.

The skin of the injured cheek which lay partially exposed, glowed scarlet in contrast to her porcelain white skin. She crumpled up on the floor and began to sob.

I stood aghast for a moment at the gruesome act being played out before me.

My cold, half-eaten breakfast and the half-read Archie comic floated before my eyes.

Just five minutes ago, I had settled myself down for a peaceful day. And now this. I shook my head in disbelief.

I went up to Anita and gently took her face in my hands. This time she didn't push me away. She just lay there silently crying, oblivious to my presence.

I wondered what must be going on through the poor girl's mind, curious to know what earth shaking calamity had brought forth such an aggressive and self-destructive response from the normally fun loving Anita, who always had a naughty smile on her face and a mischievous twinkle in her eye.

Well, whatever the problem was, I could wait to know.

First things first. I had to get Anita back to normalcy.

I gently got her to stand up and guided her out of the kitchen to the living room sofa. There I made her comfortable with her back against a pillow.

I started off towards the kitchen to get her a glass of water, when she suddenly wailed – "Preity, don't leave me alone."

My heart hurt at hearing the childlike fear and pain in her voice.

"Just a minute, Anita darling", I said soothingly. "I'm just getting a glass of water for you to drink and some iodine to apply on your wrist."

Although it wasn't a deep cut (thank God I grabbed her hand in time to prevent her from doing any serious damage), droplets of blood were still trickling from the slight cut that the knife had made on her left wrist.

I got out the bottle of iodine from the medicine cabinet in the kitchen along with some cotton wool, and picked up a bottle of water from the fridge.

I went back to the living room and found Anita quietly staring at a blank space on the wall directly in front of her.

Obviously some painful memories were rapidly flashing through her mind.

I had to get her out of this black mood soon. There was no telling when she might relapse into her self-destructive behaviour if I didn't take charge of the situation quickly.

I put on a brave smile. (Although I was shaking like a jelly from inside and my heart was still pounding like a jackhammer after the excitement of the last few minutes.)

I sat on a chair opposite her, dabbed some iodine on the cotton wool, and gently took her bleeding wrist in my hand.

"Okay Anita, take it easy. This may just sting you for a teeny second ---- there, it's cleaned up baby, juuuust take it easy, give me another second ------ there. All done now. No chance of any infection getting in that wound."

Anita had given a little jerk and a small cry of pain when the iodine touched the cut. But she bore it bravely and let me clean the wound thoroughly. I left the cotton wool on it. I'd bandage it up later. No need for her to go to the doctor.

This done, I handed her over the bottle of cold water. She thirstily gulped more than half the bottle down in one go

Man, she must have lost a lot of water in her tears.

She drank her fill, and put the bottle down on the coffee-table next to the sofa. She looked more relaxed now. She looked me in the eyes, not saying a word.

I was starting to feel uncomfortable, not knowing what to say. I was a little embarrassed to ask her what had gone so obviously wrong, but I was burning with curiosity to know all the same.

Then Anita broke the silence. In her sweet sing-song voice, she simply said – "Thanks Preity, you saved my life."

There was no denying the truth in the statement, so I merely smiled and shrugged it off, saying – "That's what friends and room-mates are for."

There was another brief silence, and then Anita said in a choking voice – "I'm sure you want to know what that was all about, right?"

A few tears shimmered in her eyes, but seeing my concern, she managed a weak smile. "Don't worry Preity", she said. "I'm in control of myself now. I just lost it badly for a brief period. Thank God you were home or I'd have bled to death by now. I came home determined to kill myself one way or another. But now that I've calmed down, I'm glad I didn't do it. Apart from anything else, mom would never have gotten over it." (Anita is very attached to her mom, who lives in Kanpur with the rest of her family.)

"Should I make you some tea before we talk?" I asked her.

"No Preity, no tea. My throat's hurting from all the yelling and shouting I've been doing with Harish since morning. I couldn't stand anything hot. How about getting me a glass of juice? And gosh, I'm hungry. I haven't had any breakfast either. Me and Harish have been fighting since we woke up. Could you please be a darling and rustle up something for me to eat? I'm starving."

"Sure", I said, moving towards the kitchen. "But you don't really need to tell me what the fight was about if you'd rather keep it a secret", I added.

"Oh, come on Preets", she said. "Since when did I ever have any secrets from you? And now I even owe you my life."

She smiled weakly. "Of **course** I'll tell you what happened. It's no secret. I really want to tell someone. I want to get it out of my system. But first I just need some petrol to fill up my tank. It's almost on empty." She patted her slim waist.

I got her a tin of biscuits so she could munch on something while I prepared her a nice cheese omelet, which I know she loves, especially the way I make it. (A method which mom taught me when I was young.)

I decided to make two omelets. I was hungry as well.

I popped some bread into the toaster.

I went to the table in the living room and cleared away the remains of my cold, half-eaten breakfast.

Then I laid the plates and cutlery on the table and was glad to see that Anita had switched on the TV and was watching her favourite music channel.

Seeing me doing the running around, she came over to help me in the kitchen.

I let her help, as I knew she wanted to do something useful. Something to occupy herself. She carried the plate of toast, the butter dish and the bottle of jam to the table with her good hand, while I got the omelets and glasses of chilled canned orange juice.

We sat down at our places at the table. (It's funny, but all four of us girls sharing the apartment have our own fixed places at the table. I guess it helps us feel that this apartment that we temporarily share is more like our home.)

Little touches like these give our life its roots. Its anchor.

We glanced at each other, suddenly self-conscious of each other's presence. We gave each other a quick smile, and commenced to butter our toasts and to salt and pepper our omelets.

The bright sunshine coming through the window and the chirping of our resident sparrow outside brought warmth to our souls.

Anita sipped some juice tentatively, rolled it around in her mouth as though she were sampling a fine wine, and then gulped down half the glass at a stretch.

"That was good. I needed that", she said, and proceeded to hungrily polish off her omelet with a slice of buttered toast.

Then she sat back, relaxed.

"I'm ready to talk, Preity", she said softly. "Are you ready to listen?"

"Sure", I replied. "Shoot."

"Okay, this is how it goes", she began.

"You know I've been seeing Harish since quite some time. It's been almost five months now. You've met him, and although you've been polite and never mentioned it, I know you don't really approve of him. You've given me very subtle hints once or twice. I wish I'd trusted your judgment, Preity", she sighed.

"But then, when one's in love, one always feels one knows best. I sure didn't", she said ruefully.

"Anyway, ever since I set eyes on Harish, I wanted to spend the rest of my life with him. Call it chemistry, biology or whatever. Something just clicked. Oh, sure I've had boyfriends before. With some I was serious, with some I was passing time. But it's never been with anyone the way it's been with Harish. And I guess it was the same for him. That's partly what made it so special for me. You know, reciprocated love and all that jazz."

"As you know, Preity, he comes from a business family, and he's done his MBA as well. Within ten days of us meeting, he made me meet his mom. I was in seventh heaven. The only thing that puzzled me was why he didn't invite me over to his place to meet her. He made me meet his mom in a coffee shop near his house. I wondered why he didn't invite me home, considering that marriage was on the cards. Although neither of us had used the 'Marriage' word, it was obviously implied, the way we were going around, the way he brought his mom to meet me, and all that stuff."

"His mom was a very sweet lady", Anita continued. "She put me at ease right away. Then she casually mentioned that her husband had very strong ideas about getting Harish married into a business family. She asked me what my parents did. Well, Preity, you know my dad's a school teacher back home in Kanpur. He's been a school teacher all his working life. He's a damn good teacher and I'm proud of him for devoting his life to developing kids. My mom's a housewife. You met her when she came down to Mumbai a couple of months ago, right Preity?"

I nodded, listening intently, already having a gut feeling where all this was leading up to.

"Well," said Anita, "when I told Harish's mom about my parents, my dad being a school teacher and all that, I could see her face drop a bit, and she gave a quick glance towards Harish, who was conveniently looking through the coffee-shop menu-card. His mom expressed what a great profession being a school teacher was, and went on about how a distant cousin of hers was also a school principal somewhere, she couldn't remember where. Then the topic turned to other things. We spoke about my job and she enquired whether I intended to continue with my career after marriage. I replied that I hadn't really given that much thought to it as marriage had always seemed so distant for me. I hadn't planned on getting married anytime in the near future. It's just that I happened to meet Harish, and ----- Bingo. As I said, something just happened between the two of us. Well, Preity, that's the gist of the meeting I had with Harish and his mom. I haven't met her since, but Harish has been an integral part of my life. In my mind, the question of marriage with Harish wasn't an **IF**, it was just a matter of **WHEN**."

"Well," Anita went on, "as I said, I've had boyfriends in the past. I wasn't exactly innocent of the facts of life before I met Harish. But I'd never gone all the way with any guy before. But that virgin status of mine changed within a couple of weeks of my meeting Harish. He just charmed me into bed. Once I met his mom, and what with all the encouraging words she left me with, I assumed that my future with Harish was assured. This was what I'd been saving myself for. Today, morality really isn't the order of the day, but I've always wanted to save myself for my life partner and not throw away my virginity on a casual fling. Now that I'd met my life partner, (or so I foolishly thought), what was the use of waiting, especially since Harish was so pleasantly demanding? Not that I was against the idea myself. I felt it was better that we got to know each other well in all aspects, so that we would gel as one when we got married. Harish was pretty experienced with women, and although I admit I was nervous before our first time together, (we went to his farm-house at Lonavala), he was very gentle. The next morning, I was more in love with him than ever, and couldn't wait to have his name joined to mine."

She paused and took a deep breath, then went on. "This sort of thing continued for about five months. During all this time, the one thing that puzzled me was that he never took me to his place, saying his dad needed to be coaxed into a good mood before meeting me. I didn't argue. He knew his dad the best. I didn't want to mess up things by rushing them. Anyway, we spent quite a few nights at his farm-house. All my spare moments, I wanted to share with him. That's why you haven't been seeing so much of me around recently, babes. When I'm not at work, I'm almost always with him. That's of course, when he's not been busy helping his dad in office."

"Speaking of his office, you know Preity, that's the crazy part. Although I've been so close to him and he's been so close to me, and we've shared everything about our lives ever so far back as we can remember, but he's never told me exactly how his dad's business is doing, nor have I asked him. I just know his dad's a film producer of some sort. I think the last film he produced was over two years ago, but it was quite a hit, so I guess it made a lot of money. I don't really know. I've never been after money, so I've never bothered to ask Harish about how well off his family is financially. He's an MBA, so I'd always assumed that if the family business didn't do too good, he could always get a well paying job somewhere. I guess I was too naïve and I took too much for granted. I was blinded by love. Huh. Love. I wish I'd never heard of that word. I'd have been happier off."

She gave a deep sigh.

"My eyes opened today morning, and God, how the opening hurt. That's why I rushed home with only one thought in my mind ----- to close my eyes permanently. Forever and ever. To find eternal peace. Thank God you were here Preity, and stopped me from carrying out my plan."

She looked close to tears again, so I hurriedly prompted her to carry on with her story.

She shook her head, smoothened her hair, and went on to complete her tale.

"Last evening, we went for a drive and then had a romantic dinner at the 'China-Grill'. He ordered champagne, and over dinner he whispered how much he loved me. He said this with a far-off look in his eyes."

"At the end of the meal, I was drunk on love and champagne. When we left the restaurant, it was already eleven. I told Harish I simply **had** to get home as I'd got an important presentation in office today."

"Oh God, Preity. Oh My God. What's the time? I should've been at office by now for the presentation. The client's coming over to office in the afternoon to check it out. Preity, can you please call my office and tell them I'm suffering from malaria, typhoid, jaundice. Oh just say **ANYTHING**. My boss will kill me for this. **Oh My God**."

"Chill, babes," I told her.

I couldn't help smiling although she was obviously so hyper.

An hour ago, the only thought she had in her mind had been to kill herself, and now she was so worried about missing a presentation at office.

It was really too funny.

"What're you laughing at, babes," cried Anita, panicking. "Please call up. Go on. You've done it before for me. My boss has spoken to you before. You're so **convincing**. He's sure to believe you. He must be desperately trying to call me since morning since I haven't turned up. I've kept my mobile switched off ever since I left Harish's house in the morning as I didn't want to speak to him after I ran out of his house. **Preity, pleeeeease call.**"

"All right, all right. Don't get worked up. I'll do the needful," I said.

I called her office from my mobile and was put through to her boss.

The moment I introduced myself and told him why I was calling, he almost bit my ear off over the phone. "Where the hell **is** Anita? What does she think she's up to? I need her for this presentation. She's got the entire presentation on her laptop. The clients are coming over in an hour, and if they don't get to see the presentation, I'll lose my job. And if I lose my job, I'll bloody well make sure she'll lose hers."

He continued with a few unprintable words, Dear Diary. After he finished, I calmly told him that Anita was really unwell and that the doctor had advised her complete bed rest.

"What's wrong with her?" he barked.

I had a sudden brainwave. "She's suffering from acute food poisoning. She's been puking all night, and she's dreadfully dehydrated. But she knows how crucial the presentation is and she's handed me her laptop. If someone can come over from the office and pick it up, you'll solve your problem. We stay quite near the office. A guy could come over, pick it up, and be back at office in an hour", I told him, wanting to add that he better watch his blood pressure, or else he'd be the one who'd need to be hospitalised.

He grunted over the phone – "Someone will be over in half an hour", and hung up.

Anita was listening to this verbal exchange with an expression of acute anxiety, bordering on horror. "What's he say? Is he mad? How mad is he? Is he sending someone over?"

"Just reeeelax babes", I told her. "Let's move to your bedroom and you lie down in bed. You need rest. No – I'm not listening to any arguments from you. Lie down and relax. Just give me your laptop and I'll hand it over to the guy from your office when he comes over to pick it up. I'll tell him you're in bed and you're not to be disturbed even if he asks to meet you. From what I gather, all your boss is bothered about is the presentation that's there on your laptop. Once he gets that, he'll be as happy as a kid with his favourite flavoured lollypop."

She smiled nervously. "First you saved my life. Now you've saved my job. Both in half an hour. I'm going to call you Angel from now on."

"Awww Anita, you're embarrassing me", I said modestly. "All part of the service, babes. It doesn't come free, you know. I expect a treat at a restaurant of my choice, no limits to the food. Now come to the bedroom and hand me your laptop. Fast now. Chop-chop. Then we'll continue with your story."

Seeing the look of sudden misery that immediately clouded her face on being reminded about her heartbreak,

I almost wished I hadn't brought it up. But then, the sooner she got it out of her system, the better for her.

And Dear Diary, truth be told, I was too curious to know exactly what had happened to let go at this stage of her story.

We went to her room. She opened her cupboard and handed me her laptop. I placed it near the main door of the apartment so I could hand it over to the guy from her office without letting him step into the apartment if possible. This done, we returned to her bedroom. She crashed on her bed, and I lay on Beens' bed. (Beens being away on a flight.)

Now relaxed, Anita continued from where she'd left off. "Where was I?" she asked.

"You told me how you told Harish that you had to be home soon after dinner as you had an important presentation at office early in the morning", I prompted.

"Oh yeah, that's right", she said. "I had this real important presentation in office today. It's for this important client and we've created this really classy concept for advertising his product, which by the way is rubbish. It would never sell without heavy advertising. But he's paying us a bomb. Me and my boss were going to present our concept to him today around noon. Now my boss will have to do it alone. God, I hope it goes well." She was deviating again.

"Never mind that now. It's all taken care of", I said, almost irritably.

This narration of Anita's was getting to be very much like the 1,001 Arabian Nights stories, with the tale getting interrupted at every crucial stage by the story teller.

"Sorry", she said. "It's just that ----- anyway. Well, we finished dinner around eleven. We sat in his car and he pulled me close to him. I begged him not to start anything as I needed to sleep early for the big presentation the next day at office. 'Screw your office', he said. 'There's no one at my place tonight. Mom and dad are out of town. The servants are not there either. I told them to take the evening off. So let's spend some time alone together.' And before I could open my mouth to protest, he smothered my lips with a passionate kiss. Well, I was drunk. I was with the man I loved. And I was very curious to see his house, which I'd never seen before. All this put together, I couldn't resist. Very few girls could have. Could **you** have resisted, Preity?" she asked me accusingly, as if trying to overcome her guilt trip for having succumbed and pushed business behind pleasure.

"I pass the question", I said. "I've never been in such a situation before and I really don't know what I'd do if I were. Anyway, what did **YOU** do?" I asked, determined to keep her on track.

"I succumbed", she pouted.

She really looks cute when she pouts like that. The dimple on her right cheek is very prominent then.

"I compromised. I made a deal with myself that I'd go over, spend a couple of hours getting cozy, and get him to promise to drop me home around one a.m. That way I could come home and get some sleep, as well as get to spend some quality time alone with him. And to be honest, one reason that made me decide in favour of going to his place was to bring up the subject of marriage. He just hadn't brought up that issue as of late, although we'd been spending so much time together. Whenever I've been bringing up the issue, he's cleverly managed to side-track and brush it off. I felt that if we were alone and cozy with no one around to disturb us, and if I put him in a good mood, I could maybe just get him to commit to a deadline for marriage. It's one thing that's really so important from within for so called independent girls like us, although we don't tend to show it."

"But I was a fool", she continued bitterly.

"I had stars in my eyes, but he just had rocks in his heart."

"I went along with him. As I said, I'd never been up to his place before, as his dad has always been around. Harish had kept telling me he was waiting for the right moment to tell his dad about us, and then everything would be just fine. But somehow, that right moment never seemed to arrive. I guess it must have got lost somewhere in outer space."

I laughed. I was glad to see her sense of humour was gradually returning.

She went on. "I doubt he ever intended to ever tell his dad about us. I can see now that he never had the bloody guts to speak his mind to his dad. He just used me, and I let myself be used. The price he paid was a few bouquets, a few dinners, a small gift now and then."

"That's the price he paid for getting the key to my soul."

She paused.

"Anyway, we reached his building. It's a beautiful building at Malabar Hill, Preity. A real posh area of Mumbai. The watchman saluted him, opened the building gates, and we parked in his garage. By now, it was almost midnight. We got out of the car and went to the elevator. Since he lives on the sixteenth floor, and the elevator was empty apart from the two of us at that time of night, we started cuddling up inside while it made its way upwards. It was fun to see our reflection in the elevator mirror. Sort of like a trailer before the main show", she smiled.

"We reached the sixteenth floor, got out of the elevator holding on to each other, and stumbled into the corridor. Just two apartments per floor in the building. Lovely design on the marble flooring in the corridor outside the apartment. Funny how you notice things like that at moments like these. Even more funny is how these things stick and remain in your memory."

"Maybe it is nature's way of keeping such incidents alive in our minds so we don't repeat our stupid mistakes", she said philosophically.

I wanted to tell Anita that it was a beautiful insight, but I didn't want to interrupt her at this point.

She went on. "Harish opened the door to his apartment and we walked in, still holding each other tight. The champagne had really got to me by now. He escorted me to the living room, switched on the light, and sat me down on a sofa. He went off somewhere inside the house while I was gazing around the living room."

"God, Preity", she continued, "you should have seen the way the living room was done up. Gorgeous. Tasteful is not the word. I know you have good taste and a fine sense of aesthetics. You'd have just flipped seeing the place. It looked exactly like I'd always imagined a movie producer's house would look. And I thought that this is where I would be living for the rest of my life. Sharing this apartment with the man I loved. That's what I thought then. Just twelve hours ago. Silly me. I wish I'd walked out right then and given priority to my office presentation. At least I'd have been spared this heartache", she sighed and paused.

"Anyway", she continued, "Harish soon came back with two glasses full of some transparent liquid (which definitely was **NOT** water), and handed me one of them. 'Cheers', he said. I asked him what drink it was. He mumbled something about a poem where the soldiers never had to question why – they just had to do and die. He told me to stop bothering about what it was but just gulp it down and enjoy it."

"He made a sick joke about it not being spiked with a rape drug, saying he knew I didn't need a powder to get ready for action. He gulped down his glass and made me gulp down mine too. It tasted like vodka, but I couldn't be too sure, as I was already half sloshed on champagne."

Anyway, whatever it was, it was strong. It made my eyes water and my head spin even faster."

Anita paused to take a drink of water.

Then she went on. "Somewhere in the apartment I could hear a clock striking twelve. I started to count the chimes deliberately, just to prove to myself that I was in control of my senses.

A vague thought flashed through my mind about Cinderella having to leave the party at midnight. I don't know why, but at that moment I nervously told Harish that I had to go.

He told me laughingly that the only place I was going to go to was straight to his bedroom and on to his bed. He half carried me there and dropped me on the bed.

The next hour went by in a haze. I knew it was an hour, because after we were done, I felt thirsty. My throat was parched and I slowly got out of bed, and that's when I looked at my watch. It was one o'clock.

Harish lay on the bed, gazing at my body through the dim light in the room. He asked me where I was going. I didn't reply. Somehow the only thought that was going on in my head and that was stuck in my brain at that moment was the important presentation in office today for which I needed a good sound sleep.

I didn't even think of bringing up the marriage issue, which is what I'd really come here for. That office presentation was stuck deep in my sub-conscious, and my sub-conscious was reminding me what my priorities ought to have been."

"I tell you Preity", she went on seriously, **"believe in your sub-conscious. It's your best friend.** It has your best interests at heart. When it tries to tell you something, damn-it **LISTEN**. It **KNOWS** what's good for you."

"Well, so I started to pick up my clothes which were scattered on the bed and on the carpet. Harish swung out of bed, and again roughly asked me where I was going. I mumbled something about the important presentation at office and pleaded with him to drop me home immediately.

In response, he snatched the few clothes from my hand which I'd managed to gather, flung them away, grabbed me and threw me on bed, and before I could protest, had started off with Act 2, Scene 1 of the show.

I don't know how long it went on.

After that, I dropped off to sleep.

When my eyes ultimately opened today morning around eight, I felt physically drained. I stared up at the strange ceiling, wondering where I was, then turned and glanced at Harish, and recalled the events of the previous night.

I'd completely forgotten about the presentation. Maybe I'd pushed it too far back in my mind and my sub-conscious was sulking at being ignored."

She paused, shook her head and carried on.

"I gazed at Harish fondly for a few minutes, then caressed his cheek with my palm. He slowly opened his eyes, stretched, yawned, and then sat up and gave me a smile.

'Thanks a lot for last night. It was wonderful, and so are you', he said."

"I decided that this was the right time to hit the nail on the head and bring up the subject of marriage. I would never get a better opportunity. I know we girls aren't supposed to initiate these discussions, but hey, it's the year 2010.

And it's my life.

If I don't look after my interests, who does? Right, Preity?" she asked me for confirmation.

"Bang on the button, babes", I said. "Carry on."

She carried on. "Well, I said to Harish. I really enjoyed last night as well. And since you did too, and we like each other's company, why stay apart any longer? It doesn't make sense delaying things. Why not make this a permanent affair? All we need to do is get married, and every day and every night would be bliss."

Anita paused. "That's when he suddenly lost his smile. His face changed colour. He slowly reached out for me and took my face in his hands tenderly.

He told me he didn't know how to tell me this.

Bluntly, he said, there could be no more nights for us together.

Or even days, for that matter.

Seeing the shock on my face, he hurriedly reassured me that he loved me.

Deeply.

Truly.

With all his heart.

He had loved me from the moment he set eyes on me.

He loved only me and me alone. **BUT**------.”

She started to cry.

“That awful word **BUT**.

That blasted word **BUT**.

Let me tell you Preity, the moment you hear a **BUT** from a guy, it's nothing but bad news. The bloody word was created as a harbinger of evil. A bearer of bad tidings.”

“So”, Anita went on, still sniffing – “That **BUT** turned me cold. I hesitantly asked him what the **BUT** was. My voice was shaking and trembling.

He told me that he'd never really spoken to me in depth about his dad's business. About how well or badly it was doing. And what his own role was over there.

He said that the reason he hadn't spoken to me about it was that there was nothing much to say. The last hit movie their production house had produced had been over two years ago. After that, business for their production house had been one downhill slide. They'd put their money in a series of expensive flops. They'd steadily lost all their money. They had some great story concepts to work on. At least, they **thought** they were great stories. But they didn't have any money to invest in them.

So his dad had borrowed some money from a financier. Big money. And that had gone down the drain as well in a few more flop movies. Business was in the dumps.

They now had to pay off their debts, and pay them fast. And the debts were in crores.

If they didn't pay off their debts soon, then forget the business, they'd even have to sell this beautiful house of theirs and move to a small apartment in the suburbs of the city. That, for them, was unthinkable. This house had always been their family home."

"But", went on Anita, "Harish told me his dad had one asset left which could still turn the financial tide in their favour.

I hesitantly asked him what that asset was, and why didn't his father use it?

That's when he said that his father **WAS** planning on using that asset.

That ace.

That trump card.

That asset was Harish himself.

Harish was handsome.

Harish was charming.

Harish came from a good '*khandaan*'.

Harish was an MBA.

Harish lived in a beautiful apartment.

Harish was the only son of his parents.

In short, Harish's dad had found a suitable match, a wealthy match for Harish, and sold him off for a few crores in dowry to a business family from Delhi, for whose daughter Harish would be a prize catch."

She sniffed, and then went on. "Harish added that if it were any consolation, he'd always think of me as his true bride, and maybe we could be joined together in the after-life.

He said he was sorry.

So sorry that he didn't know how to express it.

He'd not even met this girl before, but when his dad had put it up to him, pleading that it was their last golden chance to save the family business as well as the family home, Harish just didn't have the heart to refuse.

'**FAMILY COMES FIRST**, you understand?' he told me.

In fact he told me that at this very moment his mom and dad were in Delhi to finalise the proposal and all the details and to fix the date for the marriage. That's why they were out of town and no one apart from him from the family was home."

Anita held out for my hand for support.

"That's when my heart snapped in two, babes", she whispered.

"No", she said, correcting herself.

"It didn't snap in two.

I could have possibly mended that.

My heart simply **SHATTERED.**

Into a million tiny microscopic pieces.

And there's no hope of collecting them all and putting them back together ever again."

That's when the sound of the doorbell mercifully broke this sad conversation.

"It must be the guy from your office", I told Anita. "Just stay quiet in your room. I'll hand him the laptop and send him off."

I went to the door and opened it.

A nice looking chap, about twenty nine or thirty, stood there and introduced himself as Sunil Sharma. He said he'd come from Anita's office and had heard she wasn't well. He seemed genuinely concerned and asked if he could see her.

I politely explained that she was resting and couldn't be disturbed. He looked disappointed, and then requested if he could collect her laptop. He handed over his visiting card in exchange, took the laptop and left, asking me to please take good care of Anita.

I watched him leave, bemused, and went back to her bedroom.

"It seems you've quite a few handsome admirers back in office. This Sunil guy wasn't really as bothered about the laptop as your boss was. He was more concerned about you. And I thought the good looking guys all ended up as cabin-crew. I must visit your office soon", I told Anita.

She smiled. "Yeah, Sunil is a pretty nice guy", she said. "But I wonder why he came to collect the laptop. He's pretty senior in our office. I wouldn't have expected him to play the role of parcel carrier", she wondered.

"That just shows how much he was interested in seeing you", I said, hoping to get her mind off Harish and onto some other cute guys.

"Now don't start playing match-maker for me, Preity Singh", she warned.

"I just told you I have no heart left with me to give to anyone."

"Anyway, forget all that", she said. "Let me complete what I was telling you.

That swine Harish. What he said today morning was the last straw.

It broke my back.

And it broke my dreams.

And my future.

The swine was fully aware that his folks had gone to Delhi to finalise his marriage to some rich-witch-bitch, and he invited me over to spend the night to warm his bed, fuelling my hopes.

I did everything possible to please him.

Literally everything.

I degraded myself.

I just wanted him to be so happy with me that he couldn't even think of any other girl."

She broke down.

"And then ----- this ----- this ----- letdown.

He kept telling me – 'You know how it is, Anita. I **really** love you. But family comes first.'

My effing foot. It's not family that comes first with these types.

It's **MONEY** that comes first. And last."

"Oh hell", she said. "Why am I being so bitter? I'm better off without such a creep in my life."

"That's the spirit", I said. "That's my girl." I was relieved she looked like getting over it.

"Well", she continued, "after that shocker from him, I was stunned for a couple of minutes. Then I started to scream and yell at him. I abused him and his family. I even started to throw a few things around the room.

I remember I picked up a small clock from the dressing table and flung it against the wall. It just missed hitting his stupid head.

The clock shattered.

Poor clock. Why did it have to get hurt?

It hadn't done anyone any harm.

But then I hadn't done anyone any harm either. And I got hurt too."

She paused.

"Maybe it's just karma that we're paying off.

Me. The clock. All of us.

If that's the case, I'd like to settle all my past karmic bills as soon as possible. Get them over with", she said bitterly.

"So what about Harish?" I prompted. "How did he take it?"

She paused to reminisce, and then burst out laughing. "He was stunned. **ABSOLUTELY** stunned.

He just couldn't imagine that his nice, sweet, submissive little Anita was hurling abuses that would shame a gutter boy.

The moment I started to fling things around, the coward picked up a pillow from the bed and shielded his face.

That's when I grabbed my clothes, ran into the living-room

to hurriedly put them on (I didn't even want to get dressed in front of that creep), and rushed out of his house. The only thought I had in my mind was to come home and end it all."

"You know the rest," she said wistfully.

Then she smiled and said – "Thanks again, Angel. You've given me a new lease of life. I promise you I won't waste it. I'll make the best of it."

"I know you will, babes", I said.

By now it was past one in the afternoon.

I don't know about you", I told her, but that breakfast hasn't done a thing for my appetite. I'm starving after all this excitement. What say we go out for a nice lunch to celebrate your new found freedom? My treat."

She smiled and nodded. "I'd love to go out for lunch. But only on one condition", she said solemnly.

"Now what's the condition?" I enquired curiously.

"That it's going to be **MY** treat", she said, and we both burst out laughing.

"You win, babes. I won't argue. Your treat", I said.

And we both dolled ourselves up and went out for one of the best lunches we'd ever had.

Date : 20th February

And that, Dear Diary, was that.

The day taught me more things than I'd ever learnt in ten years of schooling.

It taught me that from time to time, we all need help, and we shouldn't be ashamed to ask for it.

The day taught me the value of girl bonding. Something that's often looked down upon as frivolous gossip and bitching. But when the chips are down, girl bonding works wonders.

The day also taught me not to take people at face value. Oh, I don't mean distrust people. But when you get close to people with whom you'll be taking important decisions in your life, it's better to clarify things as early as possible, rather than work on assumptions and repent later.

It taught me never to assume you're married until the ceremony is over.

The day taught me the value of honest and transparent communication in all important relationships.

It taught me the value of being assertive, and not submissive. Of standing up for your rights without being pushy or aggressive or bossy.

Being assertive saves you heartbreak. It can even save you your life.

It taught me the value of standing by your friends when they need you. Not regretting too late that you weren't there for them when they needed you the most.

Just as I was instrumental in saving Anita's life and helping her get over her heartbreak, tomorrow another friend, or maybe even Anita herself, could do the same for me.

It taught me that there are always lots of fish in the ocean, and rather than fall for and get trapped by a handsome shark, I'd prefer to go for a friendly, smiling dolphin any day. Too many girls have learnt this lesson the hard way in life.

At such times, Dear Diary, I remember an SMS a friend sent me. This is how it goes.

'Someone wrote on the door – 'Please do not enter, I'm upset'.

Friends came in anyway, smiling, and said 'Sorry, we can't read, we're illiterate.'

Date : 5th March

What I like about being an Air-Hostess

Dear, Dear Diary

I'm soooo soooo soooooo happy that I'm doing the job I'm doing. I once heard someone say — 'If you select a job that you love, you'll NEVER have to work a day in your life.' That's SOOOO true in my case.

Sure, the cabin-crew job has got its minuses. Every individual may not be able to handle it.

The hours are odd, and you may not get an evening off when you need it the most.

So if a hostess has a boyfriend who's not from the industry, then he's got to be pretty understanding if she can't be with him every evening and on Saturday nights.

Then again, some hostesses have boyfriends who're real jealous of their girls being around great looking guys all the time and keeping odd hours. This ends up in a lot of nasty arguments. But then guys who are that suspicious are not worth being with anyway. They'd only get worse with time. I feel the girls are better off without them.

Another negative in our job that I've realised is, if a passenger's rude with you (it happens sometimes), you've got to smile and swallow it.

Of course, no passenger is allowed to abuse you, but some guys can get verbally pretty nasty even without using abusive language. So that's part of the job.

If a flight's delayed, you have over a hundred people breathing down your neck, asking you when the flight will take-off, and you yourself don't know the answer.

In such situations, you become the meat in the sandwich, stuck between your management and the passengers.

Well, Dear Diary, now that I've been flying for the past nine months, I feel I'm in a pretty good position to reflect on the pros and cons of the profession. So the things I've just listed, I feel you could call these the no-no's of life as a cabin-crew.

If anyone asked me the drawbacks of the profession, then I guess the ones that I've just mentioned would top the list.

But these negatives count for nothing compared with all the joys I get from flying. I wouldn't give up this job for anything in the world. In fact, in these few months that I've been an air-hostess, I've become addicted to the life-style.

So just what **IS** it that I love so much about being an air-hostess?

Let me tell you, Dear Diary. Then I'm sure you'll understand.

As I said, our work timings are odd. It's not like a fixed office timing, leaving home in the morning at nine, back by six in the evening. But that's precisely what I love about the job. I was never a routine person. Each day that I'm flying, I go to work at a different time. It's so exciting. Waiting to see what timings you're going to be flying next week, when the duty roster is put up.

And because you're flying different timings and to different destinations, you end up flying with different crew members and make new friends. You get to know the other hostesses and pursers so much better when you actually share a flight with them. It's fun to wait and see who's going to be on the duty roster with you and which places you'll be flying to next.

And speaking of pursers, Dear Diary, which job allows you to have these great looking guys working with you day in and day out? It's like being in permanent paradise for a young girl like me.

And I'm sure vice-versa, it's paradise for the guys as well.

What else do I love about being an air-hostess?

That's not difficult, Dear Diary. After all, what's more important to a young girl than clothes? And shoes?

I've seen my friends who work in offices having such a hassle selecting outfits to wear to work each day. What to wear to office day after day becomes such a daily headache.

I've observed my office-going friends put on a dress, look in the mirror, take it off, put on something else, take that off as well and then put on the dress they'd first worn. Still unhappy with their choice, they leave for work.

In our job, we have no such hassles. We have a fixed uniform. No dress decisions to be made. And our uniforms are cute and smart. Guys in the street nudge each other when they see us on the road in our uniforms or in our transport vehicles. So often I've heard guys telling each other – "*Dekh yaar*, air-hostess." It gives our ego a real boost.

And then, there's the problem of food which office people always seem to have.

Either they carry their tiffin with them in the morning, in which case the food has to be prepared reeeeal early, in a rush. Or they grab a sandwich or a pizza someplace near work. I'd hardly call that a meal. Or if they go out to lunch to some restaurant, they have to wait in line, because at lunch-time the restaurants are always packed, and they end up spending quite a sum for their lunch as well.

We air-hostesses? We get the best of meals. And all for free. Veg, non-veg, juices, diet-meals, you name it. It's all there on board for us to choose.

And of course, we never have to worry about catching a train or a bus or even a cab to work. No travelling in overcrowded public transport. Nor do we have to drive to work, sweating in traffic or worry about finding a parking space. We get a free pick-up in an air-conditioned chauffeur driven vehicle. The driver comes up to our room, collects our bags and loads them onto the vehicle. We hostesses get treated like royalty.

And when we reach our destination after our flight lands, we get put up in the best of the hotels. Safe and plush and luxurious. Hotels which most of us couldn't even afford to stay in on our annual vacation, we crew get to stay in regularly.

And being an air-hostess with a domestic airline, I've travelled all over India. Seen all the major cities. And most of the minor ones as well. I've shopped in almost every arcade and mall in the country.

And it's not only us crew who get to travel. We get free passages for our family members as well. So last month, my mom, dad and my sister came over to Mumbai. They stayed for a couple of days at *maasi's* place. I had a great time taking them around the city. **MY** city.

And I could comfortably afford to do all this, because compared to many other jobs, the salary and the allowances that I get are pretty good, and allow me to keep my family in comfort.

Also all the airline parties we get to attend are so much fun. Everyone lets their hair down and we just rock the night away. That's one time where all the staff, the ground guys as well as the flying crew, get to mix with one another.

Of course, since we're constantly interacting with passengers who've travelled the world, and we have a VIP aboard almost every flight, it helps us to improve our etiquette, enhance our communication, helps us develop confidence to face all sorts of people and situations, and overall makes us more polished persons.

WOW. Dear. Diary.

Even **I** never realised how great my job actually is till I put it all down on paper.

And I have a feeling that it's going to get even better.

Why is that, you ask?

Well, Dear Diary, I'll let you in on a secret.

It's a reeeal secret.

I haven't told anyone about it as of yet.

But as my bestest friend, you just **have** to know.

You see, I've applied for a job with an International airline. The interview is coming up soon, and I feel I have a pretty good chance of being selected.

If I am, I should be joining them in a couple of months.

The money will be great, of course.

And, I'll get an opportunity to see the world.

Paris, London, Rome, New York. – Woooooow

And there's so many days off that you get when you're flying International. That's another major advantage of flying for an International airline. Domestic flying is great fun but it is hectic. We have about ten or twelve flights each week, working six days a week.

But if you're flying International, after each flight, you get almost a week off. And it's all paid leave.

I just hope it works out.

Pray for me, won't you, Dear Diary?

The you'll get to see the world along with me as well.

And Dear Diary, thank you so much for always being there when I've needed you. It means a lot. Thanks once again, and the future entries I make in you, I'm sure are going to be reflecting my thoughts and narrating incidents which occur while I fly International. Although I still have sooooo many incidents I've been part off in these last nine months of flying domestic that I simply **have** to share with you before that.

So here's Preity Singh, Air-hostess, signing off. See you soon.

God Bless

About the Authors

Cyrus has a solid background in the hospitality industry. Among other things, he teaches communication skills and conducts sessions on group-discussions and interview training for the students of the air hostess / purser course at IITC, the world's leading institute for IATA and travel courses. He is a keen observer of human behavior. He loves reading and loves writing even more. This is his fourth book. He explores all genres, believing true learning is holistic. He's good at writing. This diary proves just how good a master story-teller he is.

Smriti flies for a leading international airline and has literally seen the world. This is the third airline she's flown for, and she is one person who knows the airline industry inside out. Due to her airline company regulations, she cannot reveal the airline she flies for, nor can she currently reveal her identity. But that only adds to the air of mystery which surrounds her. She is by qualification an MBA specialising in Human Resources and has also done her Hotel Management diploma.

www.ingramcontent.com/pod-product-compliance
Lightning Source LLC
Chambersburg PA
CBHW030412020726
47493CB00003B/1034